I0601347

SURRENDER TO THE SEA

LORDS OF THE ABYSS

MICHELLE M. PILLOW

MICHELLE M. PILLOW® - MICHELLEPILLOW.COM

Surrender to the Sea (Lords of the Abyss) © copyright 2018,
Michelle M. Pillow

Second Printing July 2018

First Electronic Printing Feb 2016

Published by The Raven Books LLC

ISBN 978-1-62501-290-6

ALL RIGHTS RESERVED.

**This book or any portion thereof may not be
reproduced or used in any manner whatsoever
without the express written permission of the
publisher except for the use of brief quotations in a
book review.**

This novel is a work of fiction. Any and all characters, events, and
places are of the author's imagination and should not be confused
with fact. Any resemblance to persons, living or dead, or events or
places is merely coincidence.

Michelle M. Pillow® is a registered trademark of The Raven
Books LLC

ABOUT SURRENDER TO THE SEA

PARANORMAL UNDERWATER
SHAPESHIFTER ROMANCE

Atlantes, a lost city of intrigue to most, is merman Brutus's home, his curse, his prison. Doomed to an immortal life deep in the ocean, their only chance at salvation is to rescue damsels in distress from the surface world and bring them into the abyss. While mythology may label him and his kind monsters, this warrior is simply a man with needs. And he's found the perfect woman to see to them.

LORDS OF THE ABYSS SERIES

The Mighty Hunter
Commanding the Tides
Captive of the Deep
Surrender to the Sea
Making Waves
The Merman King

MICHELLE'S BESTSELLING SERIES

QURILIXEN WORLD NOVELS

Dragon Lords Series

Barbarian Prince

Perfect Prince

Dark Prince

Warrior Prince

His Highness The Duke

The Stubborn Lord

The Reluctant Lord

The Impatient Lord

The Dragon's Queen

Lords of the Var® Series

The Savage King

The Playful Prince
The Bound Prince
The Rogue Prince
The Pirate Prince

Captured by a Dragon-Shifter Series

Determined Prince
Rebellious Prince
Stranded with the Cajun
Hunted by the Dragon
Mischievous Prince
Headstrong Prince

Space Lords Series

His Frost Maiden
His Fire Maiden
His Metal Maiden
His Earth Maiden
His Woodland Maiden

Dynasty Lords Series

Seduction of the Phoenix

Temptation of the Butterfly

To learn more about the Qurilixen World series of
books and to stay up to date on the latest book list
visit www.MichellePillow.com

AUTHOR UPDATES

To stay informed about when a new book in the
series installments is released, sign up for updates:

michellepillow.com/author-updates

DEDICATION

To My Readers

CHAPTER 1

As HE WATCHED yet another human flail beneath the ocean's surface, Brutus the Warrior wondered if killing them wouldn't be a kinder gesture than trying to push as many as he could to the top. All he could do was help them toward air and try to give them something solid to hold on to. The odds of being found by the surface world after a shipwreck were not in the mortals' favor. He felt no vibrations in the surrounding water that would indicate another vessel was near.

Humans were no match for his larger size. With his agility in the water, he would be able to swim up and snap their necks before they realized what had happened, or he could cut them with the razor sharp fin growing from his forearms. Every time he was forced to see this play of human death, he told himself to be kind, to kill them, to prevent suffering. And yet every time, he could not bring himself to do it. As fierce and big and monstrous as he would appear to these humans, he was none of those things. He was not a monster.

The scylla were the real monsters of the ocean— mindless souls lost in the sea, Merr people who had left home only to be cursed to search for something they'd never find. They were shadows in the water, almost impossible to perceive, harder to catch. Brutus was one of the few Merr hunters sent up to the ocean's surface to capture them. His brother Nemus had suffered the scylla fate for hundreds of years. It was why Brutus started hunting. They had trapped Nemus and had given his lost soul peace. As a hunter, it was Brutus's duty to save the humans, as if doing so enough times could somehow atone for his people's past.

He'd been hunting the creatures for a very long time, joined by his twin brother, Demon, and their younger brother, Rigel. Their team was called *Warriors*, and they made up one of the four units of hunters who were allowed to stray so close to the surface world. The hunting teams took turns every few weeks. Fourteen days was about the maximum time the mermen could stay in the open ocean without losing their minds.

The vibration of boats on open water drew the scylla. In the old days, the slide of the wooden hull and the rhythmic dip of oars had been like a dinner bell. With the right oceanic conditions and following the beat of oars, the Merr could track the young scylla easily. Back then, there were fewer crafts on the water—or maybe it just seemed that way. Now the subtle vibration of engines combined with the great distances ships could travel made hunting much more difficult. That, and the scylla were much older now.

They were all much older now.

Brutus wondered if his eternity would ever end, this infinite punishment of watching helplessly as person after person died. Yet, how could he stop doing his duty? Out of the tens upon tens of thousands he'd pushed to the surface, surely more than a few had survived.

When his sister-by-marriage's ship had gone down, he'd helped save her father and five brothers. Of course, they'd only found out the men had been rescued after Lyra had been brought down to Atlantes and condemned to their immortality. She couldn't return to her birth family, but had managed to make contact with her brothers on the surface world, something that had never been done in the history of Atlantes's curse. The confirmation that he'd been successful at least six times kept him going.

The white bottom of the small vessel finally gave way, creaking a last warning before sinking past him into the deep abyss below. At least, the screaming had stopped. He hated the screaming the most, the sound of their fear.

Brutus looked for his brothers in the water. Strips of sunlight filtered through from above, casting an eerie backdrop to kicking feet over his head.

Seeing the flash of black and silver of Demon's long tail, he dashed to follow. While Brutus saved the humans, Demon was tracking the scylla and Rigel would be nearby waiting to blow the vial of special liquid that would paralyze the creature so it could be brought back to Atlantes.

'*It's fast,*' Demon grumbled using the telepathic mind link.

'*And strong,*' Rigel warned. '*Be careful. It's pushed me twice.*'

'*Circle it in,*' Demon ordered. '*Brutus?*'

Brutus saw the glide of a shadow in the water and automatically darted in front of it to block the scylla's movement. Instead of rerouting, the creature slammed against Brutus like an ocean current, pushing him back with such force the merman couldn't stop his body as he was thrust up to the surface.

'*Stop it!*' Brutus yelled, knowing if he touched the surface air it could kill him. It would burn his flesh and if he inhaled it would scorch his lungs. It was the most effective way to kill his kind. The scylla was small but strong, and it propelled him upward, higher, higher. He struck his fist at it, but his hand slid through the shadow like water, and the creature did not stop.

'*Brutus!*' his brothers yelled in unison.

He saw the light from above. There was nothing he could do. This was it. '*It's been a good run, brothers. Bag this one and get his ass home.*'

'*Brutus, no!*'

Laurel Paulson kicked her feet to tread water. The ocean was calm, the day perfect. The boat she'd chartered to take her out to sea had been highly recommended.

Then why was she floating in the water, clinging desperately for her life...on a freaking beer cooler?

"They know we're out here, right?" she yelled at the captain floating nearby. "They'll know where to look for us?"

He didn't answer her. Instead, he paddled toward his fishing buddy. Why wouldn't he tell her everything was going to be all right? And why was he swimming away from her?

"Highly recommended my ass," Laurel yelled. She should have demanded he turn around when she saw him grab his sixth beer from the cooler. "You drunken asshole, answer me! How the hell do you hit something in the middle of open water?" She kicked her feet. Fear came out as anger. "When this is over, if you think I'm going to give you this beer back you got another thing coming!"

Why was he *still* swimming away from her? He was the captain. He should be saving her and keeping her calm.

Well, she wasn't calm. Not fucking calm at all.

The water near her feet felt colder all of a sudden, and she felt movement. *Shark? Big teeth? Eat human?*

"No, no, no, no," she whispered frantically, trying to draw her legs up while simultaneously kicking the unseen danger back. The idea of just how big the ocean really was terrified her. She clung to her cooler, trying to climb on top of it and unable to. "Don't bite me, don't bite me, don't..."

Suddenly, a great force thumped into her flotation device. Laurel called out in fright as she was launched several feet into the air. The men screamed. She flailed as ice and beer cans lifted around her. Then she dropped, indelicately slapping against the ocean's surface. Her back stung, and the wind was knocked out of her lungs. Blinking in pain and unable to move her stunned body, she witnessed the silver butt of a beer can as it careened toward her face.

CHAPTER 2

Brutus grunted in surprise as his back slammed into a hard object. He bobbed past the surface before coming down again. He felt the unmistakable tingle of hot sun and waited a stunned moment for the fire of death to overtake him.

'Brutus?' Demon jerked his arm, dragging him deeper into the water. Tiny metal missiles shot down from above.

'I'm good,' Brutus told his twin, wrenching free. 'I'm good.'

'What the hell were you thinking telling me good-bye?' Demon punched him hard in the face.

Brutus flung back, but the contact didn't hurt. 'I'm good.'

'If you try to die on me again...' Demon dodged

one of the metal projectiles before catching another one. He launched it at Brutus's head. *'I'll throw you onto surface land myself. I will not lose another brother—what the...?'*

A giant splash hit the surface, and they both looked up in time to see a female's back surrounded by ripples of disturbed water. A piece of the falling debris struck her in the head and blood instantly clouded the water from the wound. She slowly started to sink.

'Oh, just wonderful, see what you've done?' Demon accused. *'Now we have to take her with us. There is no way she's surviving unconscious with her two friends not bothering to come to help her.'*

Brutus made a move to push her to the surface, hoping she'd come to. She didn't. He waited to see if her people would come for her. They kicked in the water, swimming away, probably terrified that whatever had tossed her into the air would come for them next.

'Cowards,' Brutus grumbled toward the humans.

'You take her. She's your responsibility now,' Demon said. *'Punishment from the gods for trying to die.'*

Brutus didn't bother to explain that he had not wanted to die. Strangely, this mortal's inconvenient circumstance of floating in the water had saved his life. Her flotation box stopped his ascent.

'*Are you injured?*' Rigel asked. He held the vial in his hand.

The woman drifted back down. Brutus jerked the woman deeper into the water. Her hair was pulled back from her face, giving him an easy target as he pressed his lips around hers. Creating a seal, he inhaled the water from her lungs to filter it out of his body. There wasn't much and soon he was forcing her to breathe with him. Her eyelashes fluttered, and she gave him a dazed look. Brown eyes flecked with shards of gold tried to focus on him before closing again.

'*It's coming back,*' Rigel warned. '*Get ready!*'

Brutus couldn't see all that well with the woman blocking his vision. With a light curse, he unlatched his lips and pushed her toward the surface. Turning, he darted to where Demon swam in circles around the scylla to stop it.

'*A little help here,*' Demon demanded.

'*I'm coming!*' Brutus glanced up to the unconscious female sinking back down into the water from the surface. '*Rigel, get ready.*'

'*Ready,*' Rigel answered.

Brutus swam forward. Demon changed directions. The scylla paused to alter his course. Rigel broke open the vial of paralyzing liquid and blew the contents toward the creature. The second the trap touched the slender being he jerked toward Demon. The sudden movement caused the dispersed paralyzing liquid to change direction. It washed over Demon's arm.

Demon growled, more in frustration than from pain, and whipped his tail back. The scylla seized several more times before finally stopping and floating. Now that it was paralyzed, Rigel could grab hold of the captured creature.

Demon flung his arm, the forearm and hand unmistakably paralyzed from having touched the trap.

Brutus darted to where the woman sank into the water. Her arms trailed lifelessly over her head. *'Come back here, woman.'* Jerking her upward, he held her once more to his chest and created a seal with his lips around hers. He suctioned the ocean out of her lungs and fed her the oxygen from his.

'This hunt has been a clusterfuck,' Rigel said. He'd learned the new term from his wife, Lyra. They had been married only a short time—just under a decade.

'*How's the female?*' Demon asked, his mocking laugh coming through clearly on the mind link.

'*How's the hand?*' Brutus answered, moving his eyes and adjusting his body so he could watch where he was swimming as he took his burden deeper into the abyss. If he were to break the seal again, she would die from the pressure. He was glad when she didn't struggle, or even open her eyes for that matter. He didn't think he could make the long dive down with those eyes staring into his.

'*Even with one hand dead, I can still beat you back,*' Demon taunted.

'*The race is on.*' Brutus accepted the challenge and swam harder, grateful for an excuse to get the task of trying to save the woman over with. Odds were she would die. They almost always did. That's why they only took people who were assuredly condemned to death anyway. With her friends not even trying to help her, this woman wouldn't make it on the surface world. He was her only chance. The problem was, Brutus had yet to personally take a human back to Atlantes alive.

CHAPTER 3

"IF YOU DON'T WANT her, I'll take her." Demon eyed the wet beauty on the floor as he cradled his limp hand. He breathed hard from their race down to the bottom. Demon had won, only because Brutus refused to slam his delicate cargo into the rock face of Atlantes's base in order to make it into the surfacing area first.

Both brothers stood naked, having just come up from the water to transform into their human shapes. The surfacing area in Crystal Caves was located within the palace in Atlas, the capital city of Ataran, encased on the submerged mini-continent of Atlantes, home to the Merr.

The dome of their underwater prison curved around their piece of dry earth while the thick base drifted over the deep sea floor. This little bubble of paradise resided far below the human world. Technically, there were only two ways into Atlantes—the surfacing area in the center of their sacred capital city, or a once-secret tunnel leading from the caves of the mermaid cult known as the Olympians. The Merr people had blocked the second tunnel to keep the Olympians from leaving.

"To the victor go the spoils?" Demon asked, grinning.

Brutus frowned, feeling oddly possessive of the woman he'd saved. Demon had a point. This woman was much prettier than the others that had been rescued in recent years. She had womanly curves. All too well he remembered what it felt like to hold her as he swam. She was soft, molding against his harder body even through her clothes. He'd forgotten how soft real women could feel. The pleasure nymphs they were issued served a purpose and had seen him through some very lonely nights, but the firm texture of fake flesh was nothing compared to the real thing.

His cock twitched with the affliction. Arousal was a natural side effect of coming out of the ocean, so he thought nothing of it. Maybe his possessiveness had to do with this being his first survivor.

The smell of sea flowers wasn't as strong as it

usually was and he guessed a crop of them had been picked from the caves to make hair products for the Merr women. He breathed deeply. The air here did not hurt them as it did on the surface.

Thinking of it, he reached to touch his back. It appeared fine. Seeing the gesture, Demon frowned. "That was a close call. You are very lucky you were not pushed from the water."

Brutus stopped trying to examine his back for injury and dropped his hand to his side. "But I did surface. I experienced the air on my skin."

Demon grabbed his twin's arm and jerked him around, examining his back closely. "I don't see any burns. Maybe you are mistaken."

"I know what I felt."

"Then perhaps the seaweed they've been feeding us is working." Demon continued to examine his brother as if ensuring himself that Brutus was uninjured. "You will need to report this to Bridget. She'll be excited to learn her seaweed theory may not be crazy."

Brutus nodded. "After I take my ward to the healer. We have waited long enough. She still takes breath. I think it's safe to bring her inside." He lifted the woman into his arms and carried her toward the opening of the cave.

"I would like to put my bid in to be a suitor," Demon yelled after him.

Brutus walked faster. A boulder obstructed the way, and he had to kick his foot against the rock to let the guards know he was there. On the other side, two guards moved the round stone blockade to let the hunters out of the surfacing area. They kept the cave to the ocean blocked, so unauthorized swimmers did not venture into the ocean.

"Whoa, stop," Brennus the guard said, the words eager. He reached to touch Brutus's arm. The man was tall, but not nearly as tall as Brutus. "You found a woman, my lord?"

Such a thing was obvious. Brutus paused and arched a brow as he looked at the hand on his arm. Brennus released him. The second guard, Vitus, merely stared slack-jawed.

"She's, uh," Brennus gave a nervous laugh. "Amazing. I'd like to come calling on her when she wakes up if you will agree to it, Lord Brutus."

"And I," Vitus added belatedly, finding his voice.

"Let the woman survive first," Brutus grumbled in dismissal.

"So that is a yes?" Brennus yelled after him.

"And a yes for me as well, my lord?" Vitus quickly added.

Brutus wasn't sure how to answer. He carried his ward swiftly through the halls, hoping to avoid any other single males as he brought her to the healer. City architects had glazed the brick walls with a blue gemstone mixture. Light reflected from outside during the day, but at night torches lit the halls. The soft blue hue of day caused the woman's skin to appear sickly. He paused to listen to make sure no one was around the corner before carrying her under a large archway.

Traditionally, this woman was now his responsibility because he'd saved her from the water. Brutus never had a ward before. As her guardian, he would have to approve her suitors to ensure she was well taken care of. He'd have to feed her and clothe her and make sure she had medical care and...

His mind raced with all the things that must be done. He knew very little of women's needs. His home was a man's home, as he was a man. Why hadn't he paid attention when the other hunters' wives spoke of female things? Lady Bridget required her husband to bring back live sea creatures for her to look at. He should probably remember to find his ward a sea creature. Perhaps the king would allow him to put a squid in the palace's salt water pool...at least until he could build a pool for his ward.

There was so much to be done for her already.

The beaded doorway of the healer's home crashed around him as he barged in. Althea the Healer glanced up in surprise from where she sat on her low couch. The home was like others in the palace, a large square living area, with an office, and adjoining sleeping and bathing rooms.

"I have one," Brutus said. "She is alive. I have one alive."

Althea gestured that he should bring the survivor into the back area where she tended her patients. Brutus obeyed, setting the woman down on a bed.

"I saved her," Brutus said.

Althea gave a small smile. "I gathered as much, Lord Brutus."

"She is my ward." Brutus continued, nervously, "because I saved her."

"Yes, my lord."

"From the ocean. I saved her from the ocean." He hovered as Althea touched the woman to sense her injuries. "I saved her, so that makes me responsible. So tell me what I need to do for her. Besides making her a pool for her creatures. I'm getting her a squid. That I know."

"Do you know what would be the most helpful,

warrior?" Althea dropped her hands and gave him a stern look.

"Anything. I will do anything. Do you need me to give her energy to save her like Iason did for Cassandra?" He made a move as if to lay his naked body on top of the unconscious woman.

Althea put her hands on his chest. "Easy big guy. I was going to say the best thing you could do for her is to go home and attend your affliction. I will send someone for you when I am finished with my examination."

"Aidan?"

"You wish me to send Aidan?" Althea asked in surprise.

"Well, he is hiding in your bedroom," Brutus answered.

Althea's mouth opened in shock that he knew, but no sound came out.

"Oh, I forgot to tell you that my ward hit her head," Brutus said, not moving to leave. He again leaned over the healer's shoulder to watch what she was doing.

"I gathered as much from the gash on her forehead," Althea answered.

"She is very beautiful, is she not?" he said more than asked.

"Very lovely." Althea sounded distracted.

"She looks a little blue. Is that normal for them to appear so blue? And she was cold to the touch. I think we should do something about that."

"I will see to it, my lord."

"And I had to pull the water from her lungs twice. We were in the middle of battle."

"Did you catch your prey, Lord Brutus?" Althea asked.

"Of course." He straightened. "You question a warrior's honor? We always bag our prey. We are hunters."

"Then your work is done. Go. Attend yourself and I will attend my patient." Althea shoved him from the room.

"But you will send Aidan for me if you need my energy to heal her? Should I remain undressed just in case?"

"Lord Brutus—go!" Althea ordered, exasperated.

LAUREL OPENED HER EYES. The entire length of her body tingled. She remembered this sensation, the numbness of anesthesia, and the false security before awareness came. Attempting to move, she ended up thrashing on her hospital bed. Her voice came out as a small whine. "No. Not again, please no."

She couldn't live through this again. Not again.

"Easy, my lady," a soft voice answered. "It is all right. You are safe."

Laurel looked into the kind eyes. Hot tears slid down her face. "No, it's not all right."

"Shh," the woman said, stroking her hair.

"I lost my baby. Please, no, I want my baby." Laurel closed her eyes to let oblivion take her.

CHAPTER 4

THE SHOWER RAINED DOWN on Brutus's body. He stood as a man, not transforming in the fresh water. Only in salt water did they change into Merr form.

He couldn't get the woman out of his head, the soft texture of her skin, the press of her to his mouth, the feel of her air entering his lungs as he breathed for her. The breathing kiss was said to be the most intimate of kisses. He could understand why. The memory of it made him tingle all over. He let the water hit him, not moving, afraid that the fragile emotions inside him would go away. Traces of her stayed inside him.

The heavy need of his cock was nothing new. It seemed the thing always wanted attention. Such was part of their curse—immortality, shifting, potent sexual energy with no women as suitable depositories for such things. Well, unless they happened to be one of the few lucky ones who had a wife when Poseidon struck them down into the ocean.

Taking himself in hand, he stroked the affliction from his body. Brutus closed his eyes, feeling the beat of water against his flesh. For the briefest of moments, he let himself imagine what it would be like to have a woman to hold, to be married. The dream caused him more pain than pleasure. The odds of finding love or even mere companionship were so slim. And that a woman as lovely as the one he saved would want him out of all the other worthy Merr men made his odds even worse. Already she had three suitors—three out of the three single men she'd been walked past. That number would increase as more men laid eyes on her.

Was this just another cruelty of Poseidon, the god that cast them down and then never showed himself again? More punishment for their warriors' vanity centuries ago? One woman pursued by so many men, the hope of what could be, the ultimate torture when that hope went unfulfilled as he watched someone else find love. He would be happy for the couple, of course, yet it would be a bittersweet happiness for he would still be alone.

Brutus came, spilling his seed onto the shower floor. It was an empty release, like so many empty releases before it. Only, this time, it was hard to ignore the emotional longing, the desperate need to be touched by a woman, to be loved.

After centuries of living, he knew that just because he desired something did not mean it would be his. There was no ordering Fate around. She did not listen to the pleas of mermen. She obeyed the gods, and it was a very powerful god who willed this destiny on them.

"What else can I do but my duty?" he whispered, unsure if he spoke to himself or a god who he was confident had long ago forgotten them.

CHAPTER 5

"SHE AWOKE BRIEFLY and spoke of losing a baby. Did you see a baby in the water?" a woman asked. "Is there any hope the child survived?"

Laurel opened her eyes, listening to the voices in the other room.

"No. I saw no children," a man answered, sounding distraught. "I would not have taken a mother from her child, no matter the odds."

"It might be the remnants of a bad dream, then," the woman said.

Laurel was in a rustic hospital, something she imagined seeing on late night television as people asked for donations for third world countries. Scrolls lined the walls along one side, piled in diamond cubbies near a small stone desk. The other bed in the room was empty.

Laurel slowly sat up. The change in position made her dizzy, and she had to take several steadying breaths before she could stand. Using the ends of the beds for support, she made her way to the door.

"Did she show signs of having a child? Did I miss something in the water? The boat went down so fast. I didn't hear...but..."

Laurel leaned against the doorframe. Two people turned to her. The woman wore a Romanesque gown, a square piece of material that draped over her body. Laurel vaguely recognized her as the person who had taken care of her.

The man next to the woman gave Laurel pause. He was dressed in a similar style with a short, white shirt that fell to his knees. His calves were bare. A belt cinched the material at his waist. For some reason, Laurel studied his chest for a long moment.

He was huge. There was no other way to put it. He was tall, broad, strong, and as handsome as an action star on the big screen. The dark length of his hair hung damp around his shoulders causing dots of moisture on his toga. Who even wore togas anymore besides college frat boys? When she found herself staring at his muscular legs, she made herself turn away.

"There was no baby," Laurel said. "I was remembering something from a long time ago."

The large man appeared to relax at the admission.

"You must have been the one to pull me from the water. I'm sorry I don't remember much after the wreck. I'm not even sure how we wrecked." She gave a humorless laugh. "Damn captain was drunk. I do remember that much." Then frowning, she asked in concern, "He survived, right? The other man as well?"

"They were alive the last I saw them." The man had a deep, strong voice, and clipped matter-of-fact tone.

"I'm glad. I'm irritated that he nearly drowned me, but I'm glad everyone survived. This will teach me to randomly pick activities off of motel travel brochures."

The couple looked confused.

"It's just something I do when I travel. I pick something from the local area that I've never tried before. Actually, it doesn't matter. The point is I want to say thank you for saving me."

"Of course," the man answered. He looked like he'd say more but held back.

"And thank you for taking care of me," she said to the woman. "You two have a lovely place here."

The woman looked around and then at the man. "Thank you, but this place is not his, and this brute is not mine."

"What is your name?" the man asked.

"Laurel Paulson."

"I am Brutus the Warrior. This is Althea the Healer. Welcome to Ataran, my lady."

Ataran? The place didn't sound familiar.

"I'm sorry, but I'm a little confused as to what happened and where we were when the boat went down. What country are we in?"

"Ataran." The man frowned. She didn't like the expression on him. With his giant size, any kind of disapproval just looked scary.

She tried to remember what was off the coast of Florida. Cuba? They didn't look Cuban, didn't sound Cuban, but they did have accents and non-American clothing.

"Is this a small island country?"

The man nodded. Brutus. It was a very fitting name for him.

Ok, so that narrowed it down a little bit. She was

in a small island chain in the Caribbean. "Do you have an embassy? I'm a US citizen, but I'm afraid all my identification went down with the ship."

"We do not have an embassy. We have a palace."

"I have to go to the palace to contact my embassy?"

"You are in the palace," Althea said.

A small thread of fear filled her, one of the first real sensations she'd felt since waking up numb. Strange clothing? Large bodyguards? No embassy? Was this a harem situation? Some tiny country no one has ever heard of with a self-proclaimed dictator who collected woman and gave them no way off the island. Was Althea like the king's first wife or something? Was this line of thinking even plausible or some random regurgitation of some old movie she'd seen as a kid?

"You do not look well," Althea said. "Perhaps you stood too soon."

"I feel drugged," Laurel answered, trying to keep the accusation out of her voice though it was hard to do. "I'm having a hard time concentrating."

"Euphoria is normal," Brutus stated.

"I don't feel normal." The room started to spin and no matter how hard she tried to hold on to reality, she couldn't.

"I've done all I can for her. You should take her. Put her in bed and let her rest," Althea ordered.

"Thank you," Brutus said.

Laurel felt the man coming for her. She tried to stumble back into the room, but he lifted her easily into his arms and started carrying her. The warmth of his muscled body and the gentleness of his hold took her by surprise, and she didn't fight as hard as she should have.

"Where are you taking me?" Laurel asked weakly.

"To my home to rest. I am sorry that it is a man's home. I will find things to pleasure you as a woman, but for now you may sleep in my bed."

Laurel made a weak noise of protest, but no more sound came out as the man pressed his lips to hers in a kiss. Warmth exploded all over her, tingling its way from his mouth to hers, before moving down her body to settle in her sex. She found her fingers lifting to his face as she kissed him back. The numbed sensation returned. A low moan sounded in the back of her throat. When he pulled away, he looked shocked.

"What was that for?" she whispered, dropping her hand from his face.

"I was healing you with my energy," he said.

44

"Ok," Laurel took deep breaths wishing he'd try to heal her some more. "I don't understand what is happening, but ok."

"You do not need to worry about the details. For now you need rest. You have been through much today." Brutus carried her to his home. Beautiful designs of oceanic creatures had been painted on the smooth walls. He walked past a low couch and coffee table, and brought her into a back bedroom. As he placed her on the bed, it looked like he might join her. "Do you require me to continue healing you?"

"I think I'll be ok," Laurel answered. Her lips tingled where he'd kissed her. She'd very much like him to continue doing that, but she was too tired to actively participate in anything beyond a quick fantasy.

With a stiff nod, he instructed, "Then rest. I will bring you food later."

Brutus closed the door, leaving her alone. Laurel didn't fight sleep as it came to claim her.

CHAPTER 6

"I SHOULD MAKE arrangements to go home." Laurel came out of the bedroom to find Brutus sitting on floor pillows by a low dining table.

"Did you sleep long enough?" he asked.

"Yes, thank you. I don't know how I will ever repay you for what you did for me, but I think I should contact my country to get that paperwork going. I'm not sure exactly how this will work, but anything related to the government seems to take a long time. I don't want to be a burden on you after you've already done so much for me."

"You are not a burden," he said. "Don't worry about such things right now. Sit. Eat. I brought you food. I was concerned when you did not come out last night, but it looks as if the rest has done you good. Your skin appears to be less blue."

She'd slept all night? All she remembered was lying down and slipping into what felt like a coma. After all the man had done, she didn't want to be rude. Taking a seat on the cushion that he'd gestured to, she waited to see what his dining custom was.

"Eat," he ordered, pushing the tray toward her. Apparently, there was little dining custom.

The fruits did not look familiar, but she guessed the meat strips were cooked fish by its texture. She was so hungry that she didn't even mind the odd combination of flavors. After several bites, she noticed Brutus was watching her mouth.

Laurel dropped her hand and licked her lips. She self-consciously brushed a strand of hair behind her ear. On the one hand, she was grateful to this man for saving her. On the other his focused attention as she ate was unnerving, and she wanted to sink into the cushions to hide. Being a woman of natural curves, ravenously eating in front of an incredibly hot-sexy-gorgeous male model superhero type was, well, discon-certing—which in itself was a weird feeling because she happened to love her body. "So, what do you do when you're not saving damsels from the ocean?"

"I am a warrior."

"Military?" That made sense. The man had the build of a fighter and the stoic disposition.

"Hunter," he corrected.

"Ah," she nodded in understanding though she wasn't sure what the difference really meant. Did he mean fisherman? He was on the ocean. Navy, perhaps?

Laurel waited for him to say something. He didn't. Instead, he stared at her with his stoic expression and studying eyes. At any other moment, she would have been afraid, but this man rescued her, provided her with medical attention, and now fed her. Despite his stern look and big physique, she wasn't frightened.

"Your home is lovely." Laurel was a natural talker and liked conversation over silence.

"It makes for a fine place to stay when I am at the palace." His intense eyes didn't waver.

"So you stay somewhere else when you're not visiting the palace?" She picked up a slice of fruit and slowly ate it to keep her hands busy. The gesture seemed to please him, and he relaxed his expression some. Is that what he waited for? Making sure she ate?

"Of course. I have a home in the country. All hunters do. I share it with my brother, Demon."

"Bachelor pad?" she teased, smiling. Demon? Brutus? Either their parents had a strange sense of humor, or they were nicknames. He only looked confused. "Never mind."

"You lost a child?" Brutus continued to watch her closely.

Laurel stiffened and released the piece of fruit she was holding. It wasn't something she normally told people about. "It was a long time ago." Then before he could ask more, she pushed to her feet. "Thank you for the food. I should start filing the paperwork to get home. Can you point me to where I need to go?"

He arched a brow and pointed to the bedroom door.

Laurel needlessly followed the gesture.

"If you prefer to shower..." He moved his finger to indicate another door.

"I prefer to know why you don't seem to want me to start the paperwork to go home." Laurel crossed her arms in front of her. The soft material of her shapeless gown pulled tight against her chest, and she instantly dropped her hands to her side. He said nothing. "Well?"

"I do not know what to say." He turned his eyes toward the door and tensed as if he might make a run for it.

"Try the truth." Laurel endeavored to stay calm, but this situation was just off enough to concern her. They saved her, but acted as if they inducted her into a cult. The white, shapeless gown didn't help the impression she was getting.

"I'm scared you'll scream at me," he said.

That took her by surprise. This giant man was worried she'd scream at him?

Scream. At. Him.

"And become hysterical." Slowly, Brutus stood. "Perhaps you need Aidan. I will retrieve him."

Laurel placed her hands on her hips and gave him her most stern expression. "I need to know what you're hiding from me. I demand you tell me everything or I most certainly will become hysterical and scream at you."

Oddly, that threat seemed to work.

"I am Merr. You will call me a sea creature, or sea monster, or a merman, and you are now trapped in the Merr underwater country of Ataran. Which is why you are breathing air and not drowning at the bottom of the ocean. I am told it is confusing, all our names here. Perhaps Atlantes is one you are familiar with? Atlantes is the entirety of our under-water continent. The land is Ataran. This city is Atlas." Brutus eyed her as he edged his way around the table. He stopped between her and the doorway leading out of the home. "Well, we have a butcher named Atlas, too, who actually lives in Atlas, and that can be confusing if you don't know him. So you could technically go to see Atlas in Atlas for meat."

Laurel opened her mouth and then closed it. No sound would come out, which was probably for the best since her mind was reeling with thoughts.

"Most women who come here are concerned with the fact we're mermen. There is the question of compatibility. But you don't have to worry. You will become a mermaid in time." Brutus didn't move from his place blocking the door.

"A mermaid?" Laurel waited for the punch line. It had to be coming. Any second now...

"Aye. I mean, yes. We are trying to update our language with the new words Cassandra and Bridget have taught us. They say it will make us more under-standable. But, yes, a mermaid. Unfortunately, we will have to drown you first." He looked somber, and yet she still waited for his laughter to indicate he was joking.

"You mean a metaphorical drowning? A baptism and rebirth into your cult, erm, culture?"

"No. Drowning is very real," he said. "But yes, it is like a rebirth."

She started to chuckle and then stopped. "Tell me you're joking."

"I am extremely serious. But we only drown you when you are ready," he assured her. "I would never drown you without your permission."

Laurel didn't know what to do, so she merely stared at him.

"You appear of a bad color again. Perhaps I should tell you the rest of everything later. For now, I will fetch the healer." Brutus rushed to leave and then stopped. "Are you going to swoon? I can catch you first if you wish and then go for the healer. I wouldn't want you to hit your head on the floor. Or I can retrieve Aidan so he can answer your surface worlder questions better than I."

Seeing he expected an answer, she mumbled, "Aidan."

"As you wish. Do not faint and hurt yourself," he ordered. "I will return."

Laurel swayed on her feet not feeling well. She watched him leave before letting go of a slow breath. "Merman in the lost city of Atlantes."

CHAPTER 7

Laurel jogged through the hallway, trying to get as far away from Brutus as she could. Oddly, she didn't feel panicked, not like she imagined she should be after being told her new host wanted to drown her and turn her into a fish. The numbed lack of emotional reaction did not take away her common sense. Drowning was bad. Survival was good. Sexy man was crazy. Away from crazy man was essential.

The sound of laughter caught her attention, and she gravitated toward the voices. Cautiously she neared an archway. There had to be someone in the palace who could help her find her way home, and there was a familiarity to the noise—the hum of a group of friends punctuated by adult laughter and a child's squeal.

"You spoil them," a woman said, though her scolding tone hardly sounded upset.

"And why not? Children are gifts and should be treated as such," a man answered. "Listen to their laughter. That is the sound needed in this palace. They will not always be young, and I wish to hear their laughter as long as the gods will allow it."

"As long as they still stay grounded in reality," the woman insisted. Laurel was relieved to detect the Americanized accent. "I will not have my boys become entitled brats. I love them too much for that."

"Spoken like a true mother, Lady Bridget," the man said. "I will leave reality to you, and you will leave the spoiling to me. It has been decreed, and you shall not defy a royal order."

"Spoken like a true king, your majesty," Bridget teased.

The king? And Bridget, the woman who was teaching the locals new words?

Laurel peeked into the room. A small gathering stood around a pool. Their legs blocked her view of the water but she heard children laughing. She wasn't sure if the Ancient Romanesque clothing was a party theme or part of island culture. Althea and Brutus had on similar garb. The men wore togas, their strong bare legs showing from beneath the short skirts. The women had longer dresses made from an organza type fabric, which shimmered in the light when they moved.

"King Lucius," a young child called, "watch!"

A man turned at the shout. The king was young and in fine shape, not at all what Laurel expected of an island king. She saw his profile from beneath the veil of his light brown hair.

Laurel inched into the room. The hard stone of the hallway floor continued across the open area. Mosaic depictions of sea creatures were crafted into the wall tiles, reminding her of Moroccan architecture she'd seen. The glaze made the light shimmer over the surface, giving life to the fake water.

A splash sounded. Bridget laughed and clapped her hands. "Well done, Gregory!"

"Douglas, your turn," the king said. "Then William."

Soon the others were also clapping. Bridget glanced in her direction, and her smile slipped a little. She glanced at the pool in worry and then hurried forward.

"Hello, you must be Laurel. Brutus and Althea have told me about you. I am Bridget. Welcome to Ataran." Bridget lifted her hand as if to gesture

Laurel's attention away from the pool and her children. "Are you lost?"

"I'm looking for the US consulate," Laurel said. "I lost my paperwork in the shipwreck, and I need to—"

"Oh, well, I can..." Bridget began, lightly touching her arm to lead Laurel away from the party.

"Lady Bridget, did you..." The king turned to them, and his smile dropped. He glanced first at the pool and then the women, prompting the others to do the same.

"You're not watching!" a young boy shouted from the water.

At their troubled expressions, Laurel found herself backing away from them to look in the water. Three small figures moved beneath the surface. The blue and green of their swim trunks revealed their location. Suddenly, one of the children came up for air, practically leaping above the surface. Shocked, Laurel realized the colored swim trucks were actually long tails. The child's green lower half twisted in the air before he landed with a loud splash.

"Mermen," she whispered. The second boy shot up from the water, his blue tail twisting as the other boy's had. He was followed by the third whose tail was color-split down the middle—half blue, half green. They both landed at the same time with hard splashes.

"Who was the highest?" a boy demanded, before saying, "Hey, who's she?"

"Mermen," Laurel repeated, breathing heavier. On top, the boys looked to be humans around ten years old, maybe a little younger—except for the small fins jutting out from their forearms.

Bridget came forward. "I know what you must be going through. It's all right. Everything can be explained."

"Mermen." Laurel jerked away when Bridget tried to touch her.

"Yes, mermen, but I assure you it is perfectly—"

"He said..." Laurel moved closer to the pool to prove this was happening. Perhaps the tails were fakes? They could be fakes. That made sense, right?

Bridget attempted to block her view. "Please, my sons don't understand about the adjustment mortals go through. You will be their first new arrival. Please, don't..."

Don't what? Traumatize *them*? Frighten *them*? Laurel was about to laugh when she saw the motherly pleading in Bridget's eyes. Even though her motherhood had been brief, she understood the desperation in that expression.

A pang of regret and sorrow hit her. Despite her pounding heart and tumbling thoughts, she managed to nod. She whispered, "This can't be real."

"Where is Brutus? He should have taken you to Aidan first," Bridget said. "I know what you are going through. I was once new to this place. No one here wants to hurt you. They wouldn't have brought you if they had another choice. They only save those condemned to death."

Laurel didn't know if she was waiting to pass out or wake up.

"How much has he told you?" Bridget asked.

"Lady Bridget?" the king inquired.

"Your majesty, this is Lady Laurel." The woman stepped aside when the king joined them. "Lady Laurel, King Lucius."

Laurel looked at the pool, seeing the three young merboys glide around like dolphins in a water show. She heard voices but didn't pay attention to the words as a caudal fin flapped out of the water to splash the adults standing along the side. The boys giggled mischievously when a redheaded woman yelped and jumped back.

"Is she under euphoria?" the king asked.

Laurel blinked slowly and focused her attention on him. "I should make arrangements to go home."

"Where is Brutus? Shouldn't he be watching her?" King Lucius moved to the archway to peer down the hall as if that would answer his question.

"I want to go home," Laurel repeated. "I won't say anything. I just want to go home."

"Help me out, Lady Cassie!" a young voice demanded.

The redheaded woman leaned to grab the boy's hand to help him from the water.

"Oh, no, don't—" Bridget started to yell, only too late. Her son playfully pulled the woman into the water with them. All three boys laughed mischievously. When the woman surfaced, surrounded by the bulk of her gown, a green tail had transformed where her legs had been.

The tails were not fakes.

"Oh, that's it, you're in trouble now," the woman yelled, swimming after them to give chase. Despite her words, she didn't seem too upset by the boys' mischievous play.

"What is at home?" Bridget leaned over to force Laurel's attention away from the children splashing in the pool.

"Are you married?" the king said, a little too eagerly.

Laurel frowned and shook her head. "No. Marriage is overrated."

It was an automatic response, one she'd said several times since her divorce. Very little about that marriage had been good, except for the ending. A bad marriage made it hard to consider even trying it again.

"I don't understand," the king said. "You are exquisite. I think you would rate very high in a marriage."

"What—?" Laurel started to ask.

"Make sure the boys don't drown each other," Bridget broke in. She gestured that the king should go. "I will bring Laurel to see Aidan."

"As you wish, my lady." The king bowed and turned to the boys.

"They can drown?" Laurel inquired.

"No. He'll just make sure they stay out of trouble." Bridget threaded her arm through Laurel's. "Now we can speak without his hovering on your every word. Single females are a very rare commodity here, and you will find the Merr men are as clueless as human ones when it comes to feminine ways. Single men like the king will be eager to spend time with you, which brings me to Lord Brutus. What did he tell you about your situation?"

"That you wanted to drown me and make me a mermaid." Laurel stiffened at the reminder and tried to pull her arm from the woman's light hold.

Bridget let her go. "Oh, no. Tell me he didn't say it like that."

"He very much did," Laurel said. "I think I'm in shock. I should be having a panic attack right now. I should be trying to run away. I shouldn't be talking to you."

"They call it euphoria. It's an adjustment period when coming to live here. It's not intentional, but a byproduct of the dive down. All I've had to go off of are accounts by those who have gone through it and my own experience, but no real evidence as data is very limited. I have a working theory that it is related to generalized barotrauma and that the atmosphere of Atlantes keeps it from being fatal. Everyone is affected differently and for different time periods. This whole dome acts as a decompression chamber."

Laurel eyed the woman. She was as crazy as Brutus. But then, she just witnessed merboys, so maybe she was as delusional as the rest of them.

"Generalized barotrauma. Decompression sickness," Bridget clarified. "Also called the bends?"

"That thing divers get when they come up to the surface too fast?" Laurel frowned. Out of everything she'd heard and seen that day, it made her feel better to have a medical explanation. "Did I go that deep underwater that I'm affected by the bends? I thought that was only something that happened if you dived really far down."

"We are pretty deep under the surface." Bridget sighed. "Brutus didn't explain that to you, did he? What do you remember about your accident?"

"Being in the water. Being tossed into the air. Falling." She looked around the pristine hallway. "Waking up here. Sleeping like I was in a coma and then being told I was to be drowned. And apparently mermaids are real."

"We prefer Merr. Yes, in order to change you have to drown. It's not as horrible as it sounds. Well, I mean, drowning isn't fun, but it's over quickly. At any rate, Brutus should not have led with that information, and he should have mentioned that it is your choice."

"Then I choose not to drown," Laurel said. "And I want to go home."

"Perhaps we should see Aidan first." The woman again led her down the hall by her arm. They passed two men standing guard over a rock slab leaning against the wall.

"My lady," the darker complexioned one said.

He left his post to join them. Both guards had on short, white togas and a green cloak draped over one shoulder that was held in place by a sun brooch.

The blond guard hesitated but soon followed. "Lady Laurel, it is good to see you again."

They had kind smiles and expressions that appeared a little too hopeful.

"Ignore Brennus," the dark-haired guard said, "my lady, you would not remember our meeting as you were not awake at the time."

Laurel stiffened. Why were men being brought in to see her sleep?

"What Vitus means," Brennus put forth, "is that you were not conscious at the time."

"I think they both mean you were fresh from the sea," Bridget explained. "They guard what is called the surfacing area. It's where you came into the palace. You would have been unconscious."

"I don't know if Lord Brutus mentioned it, but I am Vitus. I have asked to be able to court you."

"As have I," Brennus said, elbowing Vitus back. "When you are ready for suitors, of course, my lady."

"Of course," Vitus quickly added with a return nudge as he attempted to take Laurel's full attention. "You look well. May I call on you tonight?"

Laurel didn't know what to say. She looked at Bridget for help. Were the mermen fighting over her?

"I don't think the lady is taking suitors." Bridget shooed them away, and they obeyed reluctantly.

"You will think about it?" Vitus called after the ladies.

"She is even more beautiful awake," Brennus told his fellow guard though his whisper echoed just enough that Laurel heard it. She glanced back. Both men grinned at her.

"Ignore them," Bridget said. "Unless you are interested in one of them? Then by all means, accept their attention. Both are good men with strong reputations."

"Not really looking to date," Laurel answered. "Just want to get home."

BRUTUS WAS NOT sure if his reveal went well. Laurel didn't scream or cry or faint, so that had to be an indication he'd handled it appropriately. His new ward gave the impression of being a smart woman. Surely the blunt approach was best. At least, it was better than trying to think of lies as to why she couldn't contact her government. He was not one for lying.

Rushing through the halls to find Aidan, he almost tripped over his own feet. The man was always in the collections room, cataloging and organizing the treasures brought back from the ocean. Well, more accurately, he was always in the collections room unless he was in Althea's home trying to pretend they weren't lovers.

Whenever they returned from a shipwreck, Brutus and the other hunters sent scavengers out to the location to bring back artifacts. The items were clues as to how the world above had changed. Aidan cataloged his findings and sent small scrolls to the surrounding countryside with stories and drawings for the population to wonder over.

"Aidan?" Brutus frowned as he poked his head into the large rectangular room. Inside were rows of long tables overfilled with recovered artifacts. Aidan had been complaining he was running out of storage space. "Aidan?"

Why wasn't the man cataloging? It was in the middle of the day.

Thinking of Lady Laurel, Brutus paused. If he had a woman waiting for him, he probably wouldn't want to play with rusted fishhooks either. In fact, he might never leave his home again.

Perhaps he didn't need Aidan. Brutus knew the

story of how they came to be, had lived through it. He'd done an adequate job so far in explaining reality to his ward. Turning back around, he went to seek Laurel out in his home. The urge to see her was fierce, and this would give him something to talk about to her.

CHAPTER 8

"Let me see if I understand this correctly." Laurel wasn't sure what to make of her situation. The evidence of a merpeople cult was all around her. "We're underwater in a snow globe that was put here by Poseidon to punish a group of Ancient Greeks for being impious. They're merpeople who are immortal—"

"For the most part," Bridget interjected. She pointed upward. "Surface air can kill us. Well, some of us. I'm working on a theory as to why some can surface above and why others can't. Just, don't go swimming outside the dome and you'll be fine."

"Right," Laurel said. She eyed the mural depicting mermaids on rocks. "So, there is no murder or accidents? What if you lose an arm down here it, what? It just regenerates?"

"Well..." Bridget shook her head. "I suppose homicides are a possibility. I haven't heard of any deaths by murder or accident. It wouldn't be much of an immortality curse if merfolk were easy to kill. Merr heal quickly, and I tend to think that non-vital limbs might not grow back."

"You don't know?"

"I never thought to ask about dismemberment," Bridget said.

"What about population control?" Laurel walked along the wall. She imagined a distant spot depicted on a beach might be a child playing.

"Children are very rare. I don't know why I was blessed with triplet sons. Maybe the conditions of my coming down happened to be perfect. None of the other women have become pregnant." Bridget touched her elbow. Laurel stiffened. "No one knows what the future holds. I understand that you're scared, but life here is not so bad, and you just have more future now than you did before."

Losing her baby had been one of the hardest moments of her life. The emotional pain of it had nearly killed her. As much as she loved children, life had made that decision for her long before now.

"Laurel?" Bridget prompted.

"You're saying I'm immortal?" Laurel asked.

"I'm saying—" Bridget began only to stop as Brutus interrupted them.

"There you are. Why did you leave my home?"

Laurel automatically looked at his legs to assure herself they were there. She tried to detect a hint of his scaly alter ego in the strong muscles and flesh. He appeared normal. Well, as normal as a sexy Caesar gladiator type merman cult member could appear. At his expectant look, she said the only thing she could think of, "I don't want to drown."

BRUTUS GAZED at Laurel in relief, happy that she had not wandered off into a room full of men. He knew she'd be safe in the palace. Nothing would happen to her, other than the fact she might pick up more suitors.

"Lord Brutus," Bridget said, stepping forward to demand his attention. "I've been telling your ward about the Merr."

Brutus frowned. "I already told her."

"Yes, yes you did." Bridget nodded. She gave

Laurel a small smile. "I was filling in a few of the details you left out."

"But, I was going to tell her of the details." He grimaced and turned his full attention back to Laurel. Now, what was he going to talk to her about? He'd been practicing how he would explain to her the story of why their underwater world came to be. If he spoke slowly and in great detail the conversation could have lasted for hours.

"My lord." Bridget gestured that he should walk with her. He began to refuse, but her hard look demanded that he follow her. "Give us a moment, Laurel. I need to discuss hunter business with Lord Brutus."

Laurel nodded and turned back to the mermaid mural. There was a sadness in her as she touched a tiny spot on the depiction of a beach. Perhaps Bridget did not do as good a job as he when it came to explaining things. The idea gave him hope.

Leading him down the hall where they could still see the newcomer but not be overheard, Bridget said, "Demon told me you surfaced. How are you?"

"It was only my skin. It tingled, but there is no injury." Brutus liked Lady Bridget. She had a big heart and divided her time caring for her family and caring for the Merr people. He wasn't sure what she did in her laboratory, but he knew she worked to find out why the mermaid cult could breathe surface air while the rest of them could not. It was her insistence that the hunters eat a seaweed diet. It was probably that diet that kept the surface air from lighting him on fire.

"I am very glad you are not hurt," she said.

He turned his attention to watch Laurel.

"You have to stop staring at her like you want to devour her."

"I am only looking at her," he defended.

"You're staring and your expression appears stern," Bridget insisted. "Try to smile."

Brutus forced the sides of his mouth up.

"Perhaps not so much," Bridget said. "Smile like you smile at my children."

"She is not a child. Why would I treat her like such?"

"I'm not saying she's a..." Bridget sighed. "I'm not trying to be critical. I only want to help. But, I should not offer advice unless you ask for it."

"What am I supposed to say to her now? I was going to tell her the story of Atlantes and my people. It took me a walk through the palace to come up with that much." He glanced to where Laurel stood. She was so beautiful. Even now his stomach tightened, and all thoughts tried to leave his head. "I practiced it."

"Let the conversation come naturally," Bridget said. "Before you told her of the Merr, what were you two doing?"

"I told her to eat. She ate. I counted how much food she took in to make sure it was enough. It was not. I can eat ten times what she consumed." Brutus straightened in worry. "Should I force her to eat more?"

"No," Bridget said, a little too loud. Laurel turned her full attention on them and inched closer. Lowering her tone, Bridget continued, "Don't talk about what a woman eats. Trust me on this. I'm pretty sure that social rule will not have changed since I made the trip down. And don't count her intake."

"Go on." Brutus crossed his arms over his chest and stared at Laurel. She took another step toward them. He thought about the breathing kiss, the feel of her body as the ocean water surrounded them in a cold, dark blanket. It was the most intimate moment he'd ever had with a woman.

"Just treat her as you would a fellow hunter." Bridget made a small noise. "No. Forget that. Treat her as you do me."

Brutus didn't move.

"You like her, don't you?"

He sighed in frustration. "Of course, I like her. She is my ward."

"I mean you're attracted to her."

He thought about denying it, but he wasn't one for lying. "She intrigues me."

Bridget smiled. "You should take her to the borderlands. As far as I know, it's the best way to convince someone that all of this is real."

Brutus started to protest but then heard laughter. He turned to see Laurel talking to Erastos. The man worked in the kitchen. Laurel laughed harder. The man handed her something, and she accepted the gift.

"Brutus?" Bridget asked. "Are you listening to me?"

"He has not been introduced," Brutus said, ready to charge forward.

"Who? Erastos? Yes. I introduced them in passing as I was showing her the palace," Bridget said.

"I accept your advice. We leave for the borderlands immediately." He strode toward Laurel.

Erastos saw his approach and quickly took his leave. Brutus glared after him.

"You are accepting suitors?" Brutus asked.

Laurel looked at her hand. "I thought he called it an auv?" She held up the round fruit.

"Good. You should eat. We have a long walk today." Brutus motioned for her to follow him.

"I'm not sure I'm up to a long walk. I need to rest." She handed him the auv. "I think I can find my way back."

"But..." He watched as she walked away from him. "We are going to the borderlands."

"That was an interesting approach," Bridget said behind him.

Brutus handed her the fruit and went after Laurel. He couldn't force his ward to leave with him, not if she needed to heal, but that didn't mean he didn't want to. The borderland held one very big appeal—no males to ask to be Laurel's suitor.

CHAPTER 9

"My lady, I plan to bring you a giant squid," Brutus said.

Laurel looked at her host in surprise. They sat in his living room, not talking, not doing much of anything. It had been like that for a few days. She spent her time between sleeping and eating and sitting and thinking. When the boat she'd chartered didn't make it back to the dock, and she didn't check out of her hotel, Laurel was sure they'd declare her missing. She looked up at the ceiling. If she was in Deep Ocean like everyone claimed then there might be a rescue party searching for survivors. If they found the others, those men would tell everyone she drowned. She was officially dead.

Laurel scrunched up her brow as Brutus's words sunk in. "You plan to bring me a squid?"

"Aye, after I build you a pool to keep it in." Brutus gave her a small, hopeful smile. Most of the time he stared at her in silence as if he was worried she'd fall over and break. She had yet to decide if it was disturbing or sweet.

"Ah, thank yo—actually, wait. Why? Is this part of the whole drowning ritual? You feed me to a squid?"

"I told you I would not drown you unless it is your wish."

"It's not," she assured him.

"Women like things from the ocean to study. Bridget requires her husband to bring her live samples. He has never brought her a squid, so I will bring you one of those."

Laurel merely stared at him, torn between admiring his handsome face and paying attention to what he was saying.

"You may let Bridget examine the squid if you wish. It will be yours." Brutus smiled. The gesture transformed his features. "I have given it much thought. Lady Lyra enjoys a strange hot dog. She communicates with the surface world where her brothers live. They send her packages in sealed trunks. If you have requests, I can ask her to include a message to your family. Communication has become incredibly fast. They speak at least twice a year now and it only takes a few months."

"Squid and hot dogs," Laurel summarized.

"Yes. As your guardian, it is my duty to see to it you have everything you require." He continued to smile at her. It was a genuine look as if his desire to please her made him happy.

"The gesture is very kind, but really, I don't need a pet squid or hot dogs."

"But I devised a way to trap..." For a moment she thought he'd fall back into silence, but then he asked, "What about a message home?"

Laurel thought of her crotchety neighbor.

Dear Mr. Jenkins, I'm writing to tell you I'm now living in an underwater world with a man who would make any professional athlete jealous. Sorry, you won't be able to count wine bottles in my garbage anymore and silently judge me. Regards, Laurel

"Ah, no, there is no one I need to get a message to via sealed trunk," she said.

"But...?" His smile fell. "I have given this much thought."

Laurel instantly felt bad. The man looked like she'd struck him.

"Clothes." Laurel eyed her shapeless gown. "I would like a change of clothes. And conversation."

"I forgot to buy garments." Brutus stood and made his way for the door with renewed purpose. "My apologies. I was busy trying to draw up plans for the squid pool. I will rectify this oversight immediately."

"No, wait," Laurel tried to stop him, but the man was gone. She sighed, letting her body fall sideways onto the low couch. Pulling her feet off the floor, she rolled onto her back and stared at the ceiling. To herself, she mumbled, "I would much rather have the conversation."

"CLOTHES," Brutus muttered to himself. How could he forget clothes for his ward? He gave a rueful laugh. "Probably because I can't stop picturing her out of them."

He was disappointed she didn't want the squid. He'd given the project much thought—from how to trap the creature in open water, to how much space he'd need to ensure it lived a healthy life. Of course, this decision was more practical. He wasn't sure how he'd convince the king to let him build a saltwater pool large enough.

But, Laurel was a special woman. He needed a big gesture to impress her. What was bigger than a squid? With every man she encountered trying to marry her, he needed to stand out. The fact he was her guardian made it even harder. He couldn't hide her away from the world forever. He couldn't refuse to let her take suitors if that was her wish. She hadn't indicated that she wanted him to deny other males on her behalf.

Seeing his twin brother, Brutus quickened his pace.

"Bru—" Demon began.

Brutus changed course and walked faster down the wrong passageway. The last thing Brutus wanted was to listen to Demon's renewed claim. He wanted Demon to find happiness—just not with Laurel.

"Hello?" Brutus's voice sounded a little hoarse.

"I'm here," Laurel called. She dropped the lock on the bedroom cabinet, unable to open it and not wanting to get caught trying.

"Lady Laurel."

Laurel paused in the doorway at the excited tone. Brutus was turned from her, waving his hands to motion others to come inside the home. Women entered carrying folded clothes, boots and several cloth bags that were tied shut.

"Please accept these tokens." Brutus moved behind his entourage.

A woman handed a stack of clothes to Laurel before she could speak. "You are most welcome to Ataran, my lady. I hope you will enjoy these dresses we have made for you."

"I—" Laurel attempted to answer but was cut off.

"And these are inmates," another woman said, placing a bag on top.

"*Intimates*, Phoenia," the first seamstress corrected.

"Intimates?" Laurel felt heat spread over her cheeks. Did Brutus order lingerie for her?

The women giggled.

"Lady Lyra and Lady Bridget taught us about these designs." Phoenia tugged the string on the bag and reached in.

Laurel saw a flash of what looked like skimpy lace and quickly moved to set the pile on the couch to keep the woman from pulling out whatever was in the bag. Weakly, she said, "Thank you."

"Many thanks, ladies!" Brutus held open the door indicating they should leave. A few tried to linger, curiously staring at Laurel. Brutus guided them by their arms out the door. While turning back to her, he said, "I am glad you have accepted my suit."

Now that they were alone, she couldn't look at him. "You...you like me?"

Her heart pounded violently, and her hands shook. Brutus had never said anything so bold as to indicate he was pursuing her. She'd struggled to deny her attraction to him, thinking he did not return her feelings. She stared at the bag of lingerie.

"You are a very beautiful woman."

Laurel looked up in surprise. Brutus had stepped close. Only now as she looked directly at his face, she realized something wasn't right. "You appear different."

"I am myself," he assured her. "I would like for you to eat with me tonight."

She didn't answer. This man had the same face, the same color of eyes, the same build, but there was something off about him. She couldn't find a difference in his appearance, only in the way she felt when she looked at him.

He continued, "When my brother pulled you from the water—"

"Brother?" Laurel finally understood. This man could have been a carbon copy of Brutus, but he didn't make her want to kiss him the way Brutus did. "Twin."

"You may call me Demon," he said.

"Demon?" Laurel gave a small laugh, unable to help herself. "Let me guess, they call you that because you're the wild child. And Brutus is the brooding, serious brother."

"They call me that because it is my name," Demon said.

"Your mother named you Demon?"

"Yes." He arched a brow. "You think Brutus is brooding and serious?"

"Very much so," Laurel said.

"Brutus?"

"Yes."

"My brother, Brutus?"

"Yes, your brother, Brutus." Laurel went to the clothing. "I thought this came from him. I'm sorry, but I—"

The door opened. The real Brutus greeted them. He panted as if out of breath. Finding Demon in his home, he confronted him. "The tailors told me that you bought everything."

"I tried to tell you but you ran away from me," Demon said.

"I didn't give you permission to speak to her." Brutus motioned his hand in her direction.

"Hey, I'm right here." Laurel placed her hands on her hips. They ignored her.

"We're brothers," Demon dismissed. "You would have said yes."

"There are protocols for a reason," Brutus stated.

"Aye? What reasons?" Demon smirked, clearly enjoying himself.

"Ah, um," Brutus struggled for words. "For, uh, traditional reasons. To make sure a ward isn't pursued by unsavory characters."

"Are you saying I'm unsavory?" Demon asked.

"Well, no, but—" Brutus answered.

"So then I'm allowed to court your ward," Demon concluded.

"No. I didn't say that." Brutus looked as if he might punch his brother.

"See. No brooding," Demon told Laurel, clearly aware of exactly how much he was aggravating his twin. "Though he does look irritated."

Brutus glanced at her and then Demon and then the pile of clothes. "You accepted his gift."

"Yes," Laurel's heartbeat quickened when Brutus stared at her.

Demon grinned. "Irritated and possessive."

"But it was an accident," Laurel explained, ignoring Demon as she endeavored to defuse the situation. "I thought he was you."

Demon's expression fell, but she still saw the sparkle of mischief in his eyes. "So you are not giving me permission to pursue you?"

"Pursue? No. I don't wish to be pursued." Laurel eyed the brothers helplessly. Brutus frowned. Demon gave her a devilish smirk behind his twin's back.

"You have your answer." Brutus opened the door and grabbed his brother by the arm to shove him out of the house.

Demon laughed. "Ah, come on, let me try again. I—"

Brutus slammed the door in Demon's face.

"Welcome to the family, Lady Laurel," Demon yelled through the door. "You will make Brutus a fine wife."

CHAPTER 10

Brutus had never wanted to punch his twin so much in his life. He should have known Demon was up to mischief when the tailor said the man bought every piece of clothing he had available—down to the new style of lady intimates. Such a purchase was unlike Demon. He wouldn't buy elaborate gifts for a woman who had not officially agreed to accept his suit.

"Did he say we're married?" Laurel's voice was a soft whisper.

Brutus couldn't bring himself to answer her. How could he trust himself to speak? He didn't wish to lie, and yet somehow confessing that she invaded every one of his thoughts seemed imprudent.

"Are we married?" she asked louder.

"No." It wasn't a lie. They weren't married, but he wanted to be. Desperately. If anyone should have been able to sense just how much he wanted Laurel, it would have been Demon.

"Why would he say that?"

Brutus wished she'd stop asking questions.

He knows I want you.

I can think of nothing else. I want to kiss you. I want to see you smile. I want to touch you as I did in the ocean, the press of your body to mine, the touch of your mouth, the air from your lungs entering me as I breathe for us both.

I want to breathe you inside me once more. I want that connection.

I want to marry you.

I want to breathe you in for the rest of my eternity.

The surety of his feelings surprised and frightened him.

Let me love you.

Please, let me love you.

"Brutus? Why are you looking at me like that? I didn't know the gifts came from your brother. He stood behind the seamstresses or had his back turned. He sounded like you. He looked like you. I thought he was you. He came with clothes. You left to get clothes." Laurel inched closer. "When I saw his face, I knew it wasn't you."

"Please, let..." Brutus tried to express what he was feeling. He moved to stand before her.

"Let?"

"Please, let me..." Brutus couldn't finish with words, so instead he cupped her face and drew her mouth to his. For a long moment, he held her to his lips, not moving, unsure how she would react. When he pulled back, he found her eyes wide as she stared at him. "Please, let me."

Slowly, Laurel nodded. She lifted her hands to his cheeks and pulled him down so he could kiss her again. This time her mouth stirred, prompting him to mimic her movements. The gentle crush of her lips, the moist tip of her tongue, the soft moan in the back of her throat—all of it enthralled him.

He started to touch her but then stopped. She was not a mindless pleasure nymph to be controlled by him. Plus, she was soft and delicate. He remembered how her body pressed into his as he swam the ocean.

"Are we breaking some kind of cultural rule?" Laurel asked against his mouth.

Brutus shook his head in denial. "No. You are my ward, but you also said your intention to be with me."

He took a quick step back. "Unless you are feeling forced to decide?"

Laurel gave a small chuckle. "Forced?"

"You laugh?"

"Trust me, Brutus, the last thing I feel is forced." Laurel took his hand and led him toward his bedroom.

CHAPTER 11

LAUREL WASN'T sure what she was thinking. Everything that had happened was so surreal. She was in an underwater world with a man who made her feel more alive than any other moment in her life. Strangely, she didn't miss her other life. She'd spent most of her time planning a vacation, hoping for an adventure, only to go home and start the process over again. Now she was living an adventure, and she didn't want the vacation to end.

She led Brutus into the bedroom before pulling the shapeless gown over her head and tossing it aside. Instead of standing naked and on display, she instantly turned to resume kissing him. The attraction she had for him was unmistakable, and she saw no reason to deny it. The hesitance in his lips only made her want him more.

His touch was gentle as if a feather was placed between his skin and hers. He skimmed his fingers over her sides and hips, tickling her flesh. She pressed more fully against him.

Laurel tugged at his clothing, somehow managing to strip him. His lips left hers, and she gasped for breath. Energy hummed between them as if connecting his nerves to hers, making her flesh sensitive to the touch.

Brutus looked down between their bodies. His hands touched her but didn't hold her. She felt the arousal lifting against her, so she knew he wanted her. Yet, he still hesitated to hug her tight, to sweep her onto her back, to crush her in kisses, and press her in passion.

The muscles of his arms were tense. His chest rose with heavy breath. He parted his lips as if he'd speak, but no words came out.

"Brutus?" she asked, unsure.

"You are so..."

Every insecurity she'd ever had hit her at once. She loved her curvy body, but she wasn't an exhibitionist. Her stomach knotted slightly as she waited for him to finish his thought.

"Fragile." He traced his fingers down her arms.

Laurel gave a small smile. "I'm not so fragile."

"You're delicate." He continued to lightly touch her.

"I'm not so delicate."

"I'm afraid I will break you." He looked so sincere that she had to stop herself from laughing.

"I'm not so breakable." Laurel reached for his hands and pulled them to her hips. She pressed them firmly to her skin and inhaled sharply at the pleasure of his touch. As if he'd been waiting for permission, he grabbed her ass and lifted her up against him. His lips assaulted hers like a man starved. He moaned into her mouth.

Laurel gasped in surprise as she fell backward onto the bed only to bounce on the soft mattress. Brutus came over her, not stopping his exploration of her body. Hot kisses and desperate hands made a haphazard journey over her flesh. Her breasts fascinated him, and he suctioned his mouth around her nipples. All coherent reasoning left her. Every place they made contact tingled.

"You are so soft," he observed. He squeezed her breast. "And moldable to my fingers."

Laurel could only assume it was a compliment by the breathless way he spoke. His legs had hers trapped shut. She hit her outer thigh against his until finally he lifted his legs to settle between hers. The first brush of his cock against her sex caused her to tense in anticipation.

"You are softer than a nymph," he whispered, still concentrating on her chest.

Foreplay was great, but Laurel could hardly stand waiting for that perfect moment when his body would slide into hers. She wiggled her hips, trying to entice him to thrust. She hooked a leg behind his thigh to force him to her. It was no use. He was way too strong for her to maneuver.

He licked a nipple and pulled away to see the response, only to do it again on the opposite side. When Laurel couldn't take any more of his sweet torture, she grabbed his face and pulled his lips back to her mouth. Without meaning to hurt him, she clawed his hips and drew him against her. Her legs worked restlessly along his.

She reached between their bodies and took hold of his cock. His mouth stopped as her fingers wrapped his arousal. Laurel guided him to her body. For all his brute strength, he was incredibly gentle. She slipped the tip of his erection along her sex.

Brutus held his breath and didn't move as she thrust up. She grabbed his hips and pulled, enjoying the slow glide of his body into hers. The humming energy coming from his hands and mouth caused an intense need to erupt inside her. She needed more.

Somehow she managed to force him onto his back. He didn't protest as she rode him. His hands moved from her breasts to her hips and back up again. His stomach flexed beneath her as he lifted to meet her thrusts. It didn't take long before the pleasure overtook her and she was finding a jerking release. Brutus met his climax seconds later with a loud animalistic sound that could surely be heard beyond the walls of his home.

Laurel collapsed next to him on the smaller bed. She breathed hard, too stunned by her intense climax to move.

"You do not speak," he said after a long moment. "Have I hurt you? I tried not to treat you like a nymph."

She resisted a small laugh. Her silence was simply the pleasure of the aftermath, and she was still trying to catch her breath. "Give a girl a minute to recover."

"I have injured you." Brutus rolled up, looking horrified. He would have leaped out of the bed if she didn't grab hold of his bicep to stop him. "I never meant to—"

"You didn't hurt me," Laurel said. "It was very nice."

"Nice?" He studied her face.

"Wonderful."

"Wonderful?"

This time, she did chuckle. "What do you want me to say? You were a sex god?"

"Oh, I am not a god," Brutus assured her. "I would never be that cruel."

"Brutus?"

"Yes."

"May I ask you something?"

"Of course."

"Can you lay back down and stop talking now?" Laurel smiled at him. "Please?"

He nodded and lay on his back. Brutus lifted a hand and let it hover over her thigh in indecision before placing it gently on her leg.

She took several deep breaths, feeling her heart slow and body cool. After some time had passed, she asked, "What's in the locked cabinet?"

He didn't answer.

"Brutus?"

"Should I speak now?" he inquired.

Laurel nodded her head. "Yes, please."

"My pleasure nymph. All hunters are issued one

to help with the affliction when we come out of the ocean."

"Pleasure nymph? Is that like a sex toy?" Laurel asked.

"It is a receptacle for the affliction."

She turned to face him, propping up on an elbow. He rested on his back. "May I see this receptacle for the affliction?"

"You wish to use the pleasure nymph? But it is not intended for females." Brutus sat up. "I did not pleasure you correctly? You require servicing?"

"Yes. Servicing. Because I'm like a car."

"I do not understand what that means."

"It was a bad joke," Laurel said. "I don't need to be serviced. I simply wanted to see what secrets are hidden in the cabinet."

Brutus looked unsure but finally nodded. He crossed the room naked. Laurel pulled the bedcovers over her body. She watched his firm legs and ass, mesmerized by the way his muscles moved beneath his skin. There was something very intimate and erotic about that moment. She held the covers tight to her chest. He was so free with his nudity, unconcerned where her eyes might be looking. And why wouldn't he be confident?

Brutus took a key from on top of the cabinet and

unlocked the door. He opened it and stepped aside. "I will not keep secrets."

A life-sized doll hung on the cabinet door, her knees pulled up to her chest. The doll's head was bald and her eyes closed. Other sex toys lined the shelves, all made for male use.

Laurel deliberately touched her hair.

"Oh." Brutus reached to the shelf, grabbed a disc and clicked it into a slot on the doll's neck. Red hair grew from the head. Next he placed a green disc in the doll's temple and green eyes opened.

"That's, ah..." Laurel slowly stood, taking the bedding with her.

"To help the affliction," Brutus stated. He pulled the hair and eye discs and tossed them onto the shelf before shutting the door. The action kept her from examining the doll more closely, not that she needed to. "But now I have you to help with that."

There were so many ways she could answer his statement. She could be offended at his presumption, upset at his reference to her being a receptacle for his passions, or flattered he wanted to have sex with her again. Instead, she saw his expression, so open and earnest and...hopeful. The unasked questions in his vulnerable eyes caused her to nod as if he's simply stated a fact she agreed with.

"Come back to bed," she said, leading the way. She lay down and lifted the covers so he could join her under them. "You saved my life. I probably haven't thanked you for that."

When he settled next to her, she traced her finger along his bottom lip.

"You have." Brutus rested on his side, staring into her dark eyes. "Did I do the right thing bringing you down here? I wouldn't have if I'd thought you could survive in the ocean. I need you to know that if there were a chance, I would not have condemned you to my world. I recognize how much you left behind. Aside from Lady Bridget's miracle triplets, we do not have children, and you said—"

"No," Laurel shook her head in denial and ran her fingertip along the edge of his top lip. "My ability to have children was taken from me long before you rescued me. I know babies are not in my future. My daughter died the day she was born, and with her my ability to have children. When it happened, my now ex-husband was sleeping with another woman. We divorced and they now have three boys."

"Then he is a fool and was not the man you belong with." Brutus's breath caressed her exploring finger. "I am sorry about your daughter. I see your pain when you speak of it."

Laurel nodded. She kept her finger against his mouth as she kissed him briefly. "Thank you for saving me. I didn't leave anything worth keeping behind. I've been lost, looking for any experience to fill the void. Being here is an adventure, but it's also a new beginning."

"I want you to be happy," he said. "Anything you need, tell me. Please. If it is within my power to give it to you, I will."

"Like a squid?" she teased.

"Yes. A squid. Clothes. Food. A castle. Anything."

"How about another kiss?" She snuggled against him.

"Anything, my lady." Brutus pulled her close and kissed her.

CHAPTER 12

A TINY VIBRATION worked its way along Laurel's body. She gave a sleepy chuckle and thought, *Again?*

Brutus was insatiable.

The vibration stopped, and she let her mind drift in that beautiful place between awake and sleep. Unsure how much time had passed, the vibration started again. This time, it was so intense it shook the bed.

Laurel's brain took a few moments to process what was happening. But when it did, she sat up in full panic mode. "Earthquake!"

Brutus sprang up from the bed and looked around as if the walls of the room would give him answers. The pleasure nymph's cabinet opened, and the creepy sex doll fell onto the floor. It vibrated on the ground as if it was having a seizure.

Laurel held on to the mattress. "Is this normal? Please say this is normal."

Brutus didn't answer. The vibrations subsided.

"Brutus? Why didn't you answer? Is that normal?"

"I cannot lie to you," he said. "I cannot tell you it is normal."

"So it's rare?" she insisted, hoping there was an explanation.

"No," he answered. "It has never happened."

The vibrations started again, like someone hitting the side of the room. The initial big shake was followed by smaller tremors. Laurel looked up in panic. They were under the water in a dome. What if the dome cracked?

"Come." Brutus took her by the arm and started to lead her out of the room naked.

"Wait." She jerked from his grasp and grabbed her clothing from the night before. Then, she tossed him his toga.

"I must find out what is happening," he stated, not bothering to dress as he instead carried his clothing in a balled fist.

The vibrations subsided once more. Laurel

expected to see the palace halls filled with panicked people. Instead, several men strode through the halls in determination.

"Caderyn, Iason, Rigel, to the countryside to check the dome." The king pointed at the men as he spoke. "Solon, check the villagers and then those in the countryside."

The men took off as ordered. The vibrations came in steady waves, a heavy hit and then the aftermath.

"That leaves the water," Brutus said.

"You and Demon, go," the king ordered. "Take Brennus and Vitus with you. They should be at their post."

Demon jogged ahead of them toward the surfacing area.

Brutus gestured that Laurel should follow him. He handed her his clothing and continued on naked. "Stay in the palace unless the king tells you it's not safe. If I do not return, he will become your guardian, or will find you someone suitable."

"What do you mean if you don't return?" Laurel demanded. Her heart beat faster. Demon helped the two guards move the boulder blocking the exit. "Don't go if you think you won't return."

"Brutus, come," Demon yelled. His clothes flew

behind him as he led Vitus and Brennus into the surfacing area. Brennus carried a torch into the darkened space. She had a feeling it was more for her than for himself.

"Brutus, don't go if it's dangerous." Laurel followed him through the round door into a cave. The air instantly felt cool and damp compared to the palace. Rough gemstones protruded from the cave's walls. She lifted her hand to the stone to steady herself as the ground again shook.

"Your concern is—" Brutus began.

"Brother, now!" Demon's yell was followed by three distinct splashes.

"I have to. It's my duty." He quickly cupped her cheeks and gave her a kiss. "Go back into the palace. Listen to the king. He'll protect you."

"But—*ah*." Laurel gasped as Brutus dove into the darkness at the edge of the cave. A splash sounded as he broke the water's surface.

"Brutus, wait," she called. "How long will you be?"

'As long as it takes.'

She heard the words in her head and frowned, confident her mind had answered her. "Damn it, Brutus."

'*Do not be angry with me,*' he said. The telepathic words were clear.

'*Are you in my head?*' Laurel thought.

'*We're connected,*' he answered.

'*You're mated to my brother,*' Demon interrupted, his tone sounded exasperated. '*Stop clogging the mind link. We have work to do.*'

'*Now go away from the water. Find the king. Be safe.*' Brutus ordered.

'*But, can everyone read my mind?*' Laurel asked, trying not to think of all the things she didn't want everyone seeing.

'*Oh, I did not want to see my brother like that!*' Demon protested.

'*What? No!*' Laurel pressed her hands to her temples.

'*Leave her be, Demon,*" Brutus said. '*Laurel, he is teasing you. We can only hear the thoughts you direct at us. I will teach you when I return.*"

Laurel hugged her arms to her stomach and stared at the dark water. '*Just make sure you return.*'

CHAPTER 13

Brutus didn't like the look Laurel gave him as he went into the abyss. The uncertainty could only mean he'd done something wrong. He must have forgotten to do or say something.

Demon jerked his arm to the side. '*Watch it.*'

Water current pushed against him as the guard worm swam from his home beneath the outcropping of rock that made the dome's base. The water vibrated, but the quaking was not as bad as it was inside the dome. They swam away from Atlantes, over the underwater field of sea grass, to get a better view of their home.

'*Where are all the sea creatures?*' Vitus asked.

Brutus shared a look with his twin. That was a good question.

The guards were not as strong of swimmers as the brothers. Not many Merr were let out into Deep Ocean and did not get the open water swimming practice. It was dark in the water, but he his vision cut through the cold depths with ease.

'Vitus, come with me. We'll check the dome,' Brutus said. *'Brennus, go with Demon and check the other direction. We'll sweep around and meet along the other side. Brennus and Vitus stay low near the base. Demon and I will swim along the top.'*

Demon nodded in agreement. The guards were quite capable, but the brothers did not want them alone in the ocean. There were too many natural dangers.

Brutus tried to keep an eye on Vitus while moving up along the dome. Light from inside shone through the barrier, giving him a distant view of the ground below. He'd often thought this was what the gods must have seen when they looked down on them before Poseidon encased them in their living tomb and banished them beneath the waves.

Laurel was down there, beyond the treetops and palace walls. Days and nights fell over the enchanted country just as it had before the curse. Instead of stars, the heat of the dome attracted creatures whose bioluminescence would dance around the dome to mimic the night sky.

Brutus placed his hand on the solid dome and felt it quake. *'Vitus, join me. The vibrations are coming from ahead.'*

The guard swam straight up from below. Dome light glowed over them, revealing Vitus's worried expression. *'Is this the end?'*

Brutus heard the man's fear through the mind link. *'We need to find the source.'*

'We all knew the dome would not hold forever,' Vitus continued. *'What happens when it breaks? We all shift and become lost in the ocean? We become... like them?'*

The last was a mere whisper. Brutus knew Vitus's fear was founded. The Merr could not survive on the surface. They needed the dome. Without it, they would be forced out into the water where the dark ocean would creep in on their souls. They'd try to hold onto sanity, to each other. They would try, and they would fail. There was only one fate for them in the ocean. They would become the thing he hunted. They would become scylla.

Brutus could not let that happen. He would not be the thing that caused so much human death. And then there was Laurel. Had his saving her ultimately condemned her?

'*If you wish to be a hunter someday, you must learn to control the fear,*' Brutus told him. There was a job to do, and he was going to do it. He did not serve Laurel and his people by being afraid.

'*Aye,*' Vitus answered.

Brutus swam harder, leading the way along the dome. His hand glided over the barrier, trying to follow the tremors. They grew steadily stronger.

'*The water is cloudy.*'

At Vitus's words, Brutus slowed and turned his attention beneath them. He swam toward the base of the dome. Blood had been dispersed in the water. The acrid smell of it was unmistakable.

'*Brennus?*' Vitus called out. '*Brennus!*'

'It is not them,' Brutus interrupted. '*There is too much of it, and the others are probably too far away to hear us. We follow the trail.*'

Despite his obvious trepidation, Vitus followed Brutus as they tracked the source of the blood. It became thicker just as the vibrations became harder. The current flowed against his body, making it difficult to move forward. He grabbed Vitus by the hand and redirected him upward to where they could swim with greater ease.

'*Stay vigilant,*' he ordered.

THE CARNAGE FLOATING past them was hard to witness, let alone swim through. Brutus tried not to breathe the bloody water, but he could only hold his breath for so long. The tainted taste filled his mouth. Dead sea creatures drifted along the ocean floor, floating with the current—colossal squids, sharks, every sizable creature from this area of the abyss.

'*What happened here?*' Vitus asked.

Brutus didn't have an answer. He moved along the seafloor to examine the bodies. Even though his vision could cut through the dark, it was hard to see through the red cloud. Several of the animals looked as if they had been beaten with giant clubs.

The current stirred, soft at first, but growing exponentially. He turned his attention upward just in time to see a squid move past. The light from within the dome contrasted Vitus as the man looked inside at their home. The squid didn't change its course, or it's speed.

'*Vitus!*' he shouted, darting up to where the man treaded water.

Vitus turned around. Brutus slammed his

shoulder into Vitus and the dome at the same time. The momentum slid them to the side. It was too late. He felt the fin on his forearm cut into the squid and was unable to stop it. The slick skin molded against his body. The creature slammed into them, knocking them into the hard shell.

CHAPTER 14

"Get out of my way, I'm going to look for him." Laurel stared at the king. The tremors had lessened in frequency, but they were still there, vibrating the floors. Something inside her told her she needed to go into the ocean water. She didn't know what she would do once she got there, but she had to try. At first, she tried to ignore the feeling as fear. There were several unknowns to be frightened by in her new life. However, the sensation of dread would not disappear until it had become unbearable. It felt like her stomach was full of acid that was beginning to eat away at her heart. She had to find Brutus. She *had* to. "Brutus saved me, and now I must return the favor. I can't explain it. I just know I have to leave."

"I cannot allow that." King Lucius held up his

hands, physically blocking her way to the surfacing area's entrance. "It's not safe. You do not understand the water. You haven't even gone through the transformation."

"But if I go into the water, maybe I can hear him," Laurel answered. "Saltwater could be a conductor of the whole mind link thought thingy. It's been days, and you're not sending anyone out to look for them. What else can I do but go myself?"

"The hunters know what they are doing. Brutus is one of our best." The king tried to touch her arm to guide her away from the surfacing area.

She let him walk her a few steps before pulling back. "I overheard you talking to Bridget's husband. No one has heard from Brutus or Demon or the guards that went with them."

"You listened to my conversation with Caderyn?"

"Yes, I did. The whole thing." She ignored the censure in his tone. "I also heard him say something about Olympians attacking the dome. You have four men out there alone. I'm told there are several hunters allowed out into the ocean. Send them. Send an army. Find Brutus."

"You are distraught. This is all new to you. Come. We will get you food and then I'll take you for a walk around the palace grounds to calm you. Until Brutus returns, I'm your guardian and it is my duty to—"

Laurel gave a hard smile and shook her head in denial. "Actually, Demon acknowledged that Brutus and I mated, so I think that means as a married woman I don't need a guardian. Try again."

"You mated?" The king put a little more distance between them as if to give her more room for the sake of propriety. "Then you will listen because I am king."

"Not my king. I'm American."

"You are Merr."

"Sorry. Another loophole. Not a mermaid until I'm let into the water. Still American."

"You are in my country," King Lucius stated. "Bound by Merr law."

"Well, I..." Laurel frowned. "I was hoping my argument would work."

"As I already said, you have not gone through the transformation." The king spoke very deliberately as if he doubted she would understand the importance of his words. "You will be no good to him in the water."

"What if I transform in a bath first? Then will you let me go?" The idea of drowning terrified her, but not as badly as losing Brutus. She didn't understand why or how it was possible, but she physically ached at his absence. Lying awake at night in his bed, alone, smelling him on the pillow had been so torturous she'd moved onto the couch to be able to fall asleep.

"It would have to be the pool. Saltwater transforms."

"Fine. Let's do it." She nodded nervously. Laurel moved as if to go to the pool only to stop. "Is it going to hurt?"

"I don't remember." The king gestured that she should walk with him, as he again tried to lead her away from the surfacing area. "Don't you know? Brutus rescued you from drowning."

"I meant the transformation," she clarified. "And I was barely conscious during the drowning part."

"You will not find out today. I cannot allow it. You will wait for your husband to return and then—"

"If you don't want me finding a way to go after them, you're going to have to tell me what is happening. I need to know. Why are the Olympians after your people? Who are they?"

King Lucius looked as if he wouldn't answer.

"Brutus is out there," Laurel insisted. "He said you would help me. How you can assist me is by explaining what is going on. I did not choose to come down here, but I'm here now. And don't get me wrong, I'm happy to be saved from death, but I need to know."

"I suppose there is no harm in telling you what everyone already knows. At least, if it comes from me, I'll be assured you have the facts." King Lucius sighed in resignation. "The Olympians are a group of women who do not value life as the Merr do. They are a small sect of mermaids that reside in a region nicknamed Mt. Olympus. Recently, it came to our attention they were luring human men down to be their slaves. They did not allow these men to transform to be like us, and from what we can gather these men were not in danger of drowning when the mermaids took them. We only save those who have little to no chance of survival. It is the law. If the human men disobeyed their mistresses, they were killed. We discovered how the Olympians were leaving the dome, and we took steps to ensure they could no longer get out. Their queen was less than pleased and has been trying to cause trouble ever since. It is our belief she has something to do with these earthquakes. Her followers have been found outside of their territory by the dome. Caderyn questions one of them now, so that is all I can tell you."

"We must do something," Laurel stated. "You said they have been trying to break the dome. What will happen to everyone if they succeed?"

"Our world will end, and we will become lost in the ocean."

"Then let me go into the water to help Brutus." Laurel insisted. The king motioned in denial. "I have to do something. Let me do something."

"No. Right now our task is much more difficult. We have to wait and trust those in the water can handle themselves."

CHAPTER 15

"I'm not waiting around to hear if evil mermaids attacked Brutus." Laurel side-eyed Bridget while her face was still turned upward toward the very dark blue sky. The color had to of come from the ocean, yet it was daytime inside the dome. She thought of all the water on top of her, pressing down. She couldn't hold her breath and return to the surface. If the mermaids succeeded, and the dome caved in, she'd drown. Then, apparently she'd be reborn to wander the ocean forever.

"The king wants you relaxing. Try not to think about it," Bridget said. She kept her voice soft, but Laurel could see the woman's concern lining her tired eyes.

"I can't explain it, but I know Brutus is out there. I feel him. Like a beacon calling to me, pulling me in his direction. I have given myself a migraine trying to communicate with him. I can't hear him in my head. I should be able to hear him in my head. You said I would be able to. Aidan told me that when I transform the ability becomes stronger. So, I'm going to drown, and you're going to help me."

Bridget arched a brow. "And I will do this because?"

"We come from the same place. We're both modern women. You owe me for not freaking out and scaring your merboys. You'll do it because you're a good person, and you know what it's like to be me." Laurel didn't care which argument won.

Bridget's look relaxed. "I know it's difficult waiting, and I can't say it gets easier, but it becomes more familiar. I still worry when Caderyn goes off on his ocean runs."

"Then have Caderyn go," Laurel insisted.

"He's in the countryside with the others, tracking down the Olympians. They feel it's the quickest way to find answers."

"I lost a baby. And I can tell you that losing a child rips out your soul. You have three boys, your babies. If you won't help me because of me, then help me because of them. If Brutus needs help, then let me find him and help him. Or I can find him and tell him to watch out for Olympians trying to break the dome. We have to do something. Don't let your children become lost." Laurel took a deep breath.

Bridget's eyes moistened with tears as any good mother's would at such an argument.

"Ok, fine. Don't go against the king by helping me. Just..." Laurel sighed. "Just keep the boys out of the pool area until whatever is going to happen to me, happens. I don't want to scare them. I'll transform and then I'll go. You don't have to help, only please don't say anything."

Bridget shook her head and made a sound of frustration. "Meet me by the pool. I'll bring the chains."

STANDING on the edge of the palace pool, staring in, arms weighed down by thick iron chains... Yep, this was some scary shit.

Laurel began to shake. "I don't think I can do it."

"Open your mouth." Bridget fussed with an old lock to bind the chains together to keep Laurel from moving. Once she had the lock threaded through the links, she clicked it shut.

"Does it hurt?" Laurel asked, her voice shaky.

"It feels like what you'd expect of drowning. Scary. Wet. Deafening. Except for your heart beating in your ears. When I turned, it was by force. Olympians drowned me in a pond by restraining me under and kicking me. But then it was peaceful." Bridget checked the chains again to make sure they'd hold. "Open your mouth."

"I meant transforming. I already know drowning is going to suck."

"Transforming?" Bridget stood. "Not really. It tingles. Now open your mouth."

"Will I go all werewolf howl at the moon insane and try to eat people?" She wasn't ready to jump. Not yet.

"We're not cannibals. Open your mouth."

"Will I feel my bones snap and my skin rip?"

"We're not in a horror movie. Open."

"Will I have any special powers?"

"You'll be able to breathe water."

"Will I be able to transform back?"

"That's a silly question."

"I meant, easily. Is it hard to figure out how to be human again?"

"You get out of the water and dry off. Laurel, stop stalling and open your mouth." Bridget lifted her hand.

"Will it take a long time to hap—" As Laurel spoke, Bridget squirted bitter liquid through her lips. "—pen?" Laurel coughed. Her mouth numbed and her heart began to pound. The chains felt heavier than before, and she swayed.

"That should speed the dying process along. Best I can do to make this easier." Bridget placed her hand on Laurel's shoulder. "Don't worry. I'll jump in and unchain you when it is over."

Laurel tried to protest as she was pushed into the saltwater pool. On instinct, she inhaled a full breath of air and held it seconds before she went under. She'd been so focused on convincing herself this needed to be done to communicate with Brutus that she'd not thought of one fundamental question— what if it didn't work? What if she didn't become one of them? That fear came over her in full force as the cool water encased her. She struggled to be free of the chains.

The surface was close, yet so far. The wavy pattern of Bridget stood over her. Her lungs burned as if her racing heart used up all the oxygen in a matter of seconds. Though she tried to hold on, she involuntarily gasped for air that was not there. The salty taste of the water passed her lips. Her body convulsed violently moments before her vision dimmed.

CHAPTER 16

'SHIT. SHIT. SHIT. SHIT. SHIT. SHIT. SHIT. SHIT.'

Brutus slowly opened his eyes at the sound. The dead squid pinned his body against the rocky base of the dome. Though he'd endeavored to escape several times, the position made digging himself out impossible, and he'd struggled to wiggle himself loose. A jagged outcropping trapped his tail. If he pulled too hard, he'd rip himself open. When he tried cutting himself free, his sharp forearm fin kept catching on the animal's cartilage.

'*Shit. Shit. Ahh! No. Fuck. Fuck. Fuck.*'

'*What?*' Brutus attempted to direct his thoughts, confused.

'*Oh, this is stupid. Where did all the dead animals*

come from? Don't eat me whatever did this. I don't taste good. Shit. Shit. Shit.'

'Laurel?" Brutus came more fully aware as her voice invaded his mind. 'What's going on? How did you get out? The dome? Did the dome...?' He looked upward trying to detect if there were others in the water. From his position, it was difficult to see, but the glow indicated the dome should be intact.

'Brutus?' Laurel practically shouted his name. 'Where are you? Talk to me. I can't believe I found you. Where are you? I can't see that well.'

'It's the blood. It clouds the water. Don't worry, nothing is out here right now besides us and a few scavengers.'

'Keep talking. I think I can locate you.'

'Who is out here with you?' Brutus tried to push up at the squid, but it still didn't move.

'Don't be mad. I snuck out of the palace to find you. The guards were with you in the water, so the surfacing area wasn't being watched as closely.' Laurel appeared over him. The light dusting of golden brown scales next to her eyes were deep in color, showing her high state of emotional distress. The length of her hair was tied at the nape of her neck to keep it from drifting into her face. She wore a shirt to cover her breasts, but the unmistakable swish of her mermaid's tail fluttered behind her. It was clear by her jerking movements she was still learning to control her new body.

She grabbed his face and kissed him. The suddenness of the gesture took him by surprise. When she pulled back, she searched his expression.

'Your scales are so dark, like your eyes,' she whispered, touching his temple. Then as if realizing what she was doing, she blinked rapidly and then looked over to where his body lay wedged. She instantly rammed her shoulder into the animal and pushed as hard as she could. The pressure on his tail lessened but not enough for him to squirm free. *'Did you fight all these animals?'*

'No. Most of them were like this when we arrived. They propelled themselves into the dome to cause the earthquakes we were feeling inside. I don't know why they'd behave in such a way.'

'King Lucius said Olympians were acting out somehow. He thinks they are responsible for the trouble we've been experiencing. Something about how they were not in their territory but on Merr land, and Caderyn as well as others are looking for more or interrogating them or...that's about all I know.' She grunted as she pushed harder. The squid didn't

move. *'How did they make these animals commit suicide?'*

'We're able to beckon animals to the dome from inside if we concentrate hard enough and know the frequencies the creatures respond to. It's mostly trial and error and luck. The Olympians must have discovered a way to call the animals in. Though, why would they want to destroy their home? With no Atlantes, they will be as lost as we.'

'We have cults like that. Those who commit mass suicide in the name of a cause. Led by some charismatic nut job.' She began bouncing her shoulder against the squid.

'Queen Maia is their leader. I do not know what a nut job is, but we do question her sanity.'

'Ah! Dammit. It doesn't appear to be moving.' She stopped pushing. *'This thing feels like slimy gelatin. How did you become trapped?'*

'Vitus and I were struck by this one as it charged the dome.' Brutus closed his eyes. *'You shouldn't be out here.'*

'Where are the others? Where is your brother?'

At her inquiry, Brutus directed his attention along the squid's side. She followed his gaze to where Vitus's hand stuck out from under the carcass.

'*Demon and Brennus are searching the other side of the dome. I'm waiting for them to come this way.*'

'*Vitus?*' Laurel went to where Vitus lay suffocated beneath the squid. The hand did not move.

'*I couldn't get to him in time. He was like that when I regained consciousness.*' Brutus had to look away. He'd been staring at the hand for hours, possibly days. The pain of losing an old friend caused an ache to settle inside him. '*I don't think he survived being crushed against the dome. It doesn't look as if he tried to get out from under the squid. We should never have allowed a palace guard into the water without more training.*'

'*It's not your fault. I know in my heart that's true.*' Laurel caressed his face. '*We'll handle one problem at a time. So, first things first, how do I get you out of here?*'

Brutus's idea was to have her swim home to safety and let him wait for Demon to find him. However, since he wasn't in a position to force her back to the palace, Laurel refused to leave him. She didn't drown, wake up as a fish and jump into the ocean for a crash course in underwater maneuvering, only to give up now. Instead, she swam full tilt at the squid body, twisting around so her side slammed into the creature in an attempt to dislodge it.

As her back struck the animal, she gasped in pain but felt the carcass move by small degrees. '*Did that —?*' A floating object in the corner of her vision cut off her words. The hit had dislodged Vitus's arm. The lone limb floated along the bottom of the ocean floor before settling several feet away. Seeing Brutus struggling to be free, she reached to assist him.

'Try that again. I think it's working,' he said. His dark hair drifted around his face, covering his mouth and nose from view.

Laurel nodded and again moved back to gain momentum. She made a beeline for the squid and again turned at the last possible second to slam into it.

'Oof, you did it. Help me,' Brutus said, reaching out his arm.

Laurel braced her tail and pulled his wrist. Brutus's body slipped free, and they both tumbled back, somersaulting in the water. Almost immediately, Brutus righted himself and caught her against his chest. He held her tight.

'You shouldn't be down here,' he said through the mind link. The whole talking with your brainwaves was something she was still getting used to. *'But thank you for saving me.'*

'You saved me first.'

The ocean water was freezing, but it didn't bother her skin like she'd thought it would. It was also dark, but her vision cut through the darkness like a flashlight in the night. Light from inside the dome helped illuminated the immediate area. Albino lobsters with misshapen arms scavenged the corpse of an ugly fish with a massive under bite and sharp teeth.

Brutus kissed her briefly before letting her go. He swam to where Vitus's arm had been. '*I should take him home.*'

Laurel's gaze swept over the seafloor. She found the dismembered forearm and pinched at the fin to hold it as she swam to where Brutus was reaching beneath the squid.

'*He's not here.*' Brutus reached deeper, rooting around. Sand kicked up around him as he tried to dig. She detected a nasty cut along his small caudal fin, but it didn't seem to affect his movements.

Laurel dropped the arm and swam upward to look around the immediate area. Seeing an unmoving body, she opened her mouth to shout. Briny water flooded in, keeping her from making a noise. She tried again. '*Brutus, I think I found him.*'

Laurel led the way to the fallen merman. Brutus ran his hands over Vitus's neck and chest before lifting him into his arms. '*We need to get him to Althea.*'

'*Go. I'll follow.*' Laurel darted down and grabbed the arm. The texture of the solid mass appeared strange, but she didn't feel right leaving the limb behind to be snacked on by creepy lobsters.

'*If you get lost, go to the top of the rock base and follow the curve of the dome,*' he said. '*I'll come back and find you.*'

Brutus carried Vitus by hooking his arm around him. The silk of his caudal fin and the diamond shaped scales of his tail caught hints of the dome light, but the dark color was hard to track in the water and several times she had to call out to him.

The fourth time it happened, she said, '*You swim so much faster than I do. Take Vitus. He needs help. I'll swim up by the dome. I made it into the water, I can figure out my way back inside.*'

'*No, I can't leave you alone out here.*' He pulled her toward him with his free arm.

Laurel caressed his face. '*I told the king we were mated.*'

Brutus gave a small smile, but the expression didn't last long.

'*If Vitus dies because I swim too slowly I could never forgive myself. Please, you have to. Just hurry. Take this,*' she handed him the arm, '*and him, and come right back for me.*' In truth, her body was sore from both slamming against the squid to free him and from the length of time she'd already been swimming around it the water. She needed to rest.

'*Keep moving. Be alert. Stay close to the base, but up by the edge of the light. Keep your thoughts open so you may hear my call.*'

'*I'll be fine. Get Vitus help.*' She had no way of knowing if that were true, but she knew Brutus wouldn't take longer than he needed to. As she watched him swim away, there was so much she wanted to say to him. This was not the time.

Now that she'd found him, swimming in deep ocean was scarier. She didn't have the narrow-minded focus of helping Brutus to keep her thoughts occupied. She touched the smooth dome. It really was like a snow globe in the middle of the ocean. The glass-like barrier let her glimpse inside. An old stone wall jutted from the landscape, but there were no people. Behind her, the blackness of the ocean stretched on, deep and dark and frightening as hell. She stared into the dome like it was a blanket to hide under to keep her safe. She began the slow swim back.

'*Freedom! I told you it would work.*'

Laurel stopped swimming at the sound of a woman's sultry voice and peered into the dome. She wasn't sure how much time had passed or how close she was to the surfacing area. She didn't see anyone on the other side.

'*Stupid Merr,*' another female voice answered as if agreeing. Cackling laughter followed the comment.

Realizing the telepathic sound probably came from the water, Laurel pulled herself down into the shadow of the rocky ledge of the base and held very still as she peered over the distance. She caught movement. The mermaids swam above her, further away from the dome.

A mermaid with red hair and scales led two others—one with long black hair and a green tail, and one a blonde with purplish-grey. Like Laurel, the fins along the women's forearms were smaller than Brutus's. They appeared dainty and delicate. Unlike Laurel, they were completely naked.

'*Lucius is a fool,*' one of them said. Without their lips moving, Laurel couldn't see who spoke. '*He thinks he can keep me out of the water. It was that hubris that put us down here.*'

'*You were standing right beside him when it happened, your majesty.*'

'*Shut your mouth.*' The dark-haired one slapped the redhead.

Laurel tried not to think or move as she watched them from below.

The redhead smiled and hovered in the water. *'That wasn't a complaint. I like immortality. Thank you, my queen, for making it so.'*

The dark-haired mermaid looked somewhat pacified at the comment. *'Lucius's tyranny is coming to an end. This is my world. My rules. No one locks me inside the dome. He's a fool to think he could keep me contained for long.'*

'It feels good to be in the ocean again. How I have missed it.' The voice was new. She could only assume the blonde spoke.

'Almost as much as I missed the hunt.' The redhead looked as if she would swim upward.

The dark-haired mermaid stopped her. *'Not yet, but soon.'*

'We need new stock. Our slaves grow tiresome. None of the men even try to resist my will. I want new toys.'

Something tickled Laurel's hip, and she glanced down to see a thin, long, translucent worm coming out of the base of the dome. She bit her lip, trying not to scream as it continued to touch her.

'Quiet. Do you hear that?'

All three mermaids turned their attention downward in her direction. Laurel tried to think of ocean sounds. She held very still.

'*Someone's coming.*'

The three women darted off into the distance.

Laurel's heart raced as she pulled her body along the rocky base, away from the worm's hole and from the angry Olympians.

CHAPTER 18

'*LAUREL?*' Brutus's voice caused her to move faster.

She used her entire body to swim toward it. '*I'm here. I'm here. Please, get me out of the water.*' She crashed into his arms and hugged him tight. '*I don't like being out here without you. Mer—*'

'*You told the king we were mated? You are my wife?*' He gently held her face. The words tumbled out of him as if they'd been burning inside his brain since he'd left her, just waiting to be spoken. Now that Vitus was delivered home, he appeared eager to resume their conversation. '*You are sure I am who you want? You have thought this through? You do not feel forced because of what we did?*'

When he touched her, she felt safe. '*Yes. I want to be with you. How can you even ask that after what happened between us? I felt you when you were gone. I sensed you were in trouble. I knew that you needed help. I drowned myself so I could come out here and find you.'* She glanced away and then back again. *'And you? Am I who you want? Are you mad that I told the king? It just came out, but I don't want to take it back.'*

'I wanted you from the moment you kept me from breathing surface air, when your red box blocked my assent and our bodies brushed for the first time.' The light dusting of scales next to his eyes darkened slightly. *'I wanted you when you drifted beneath the water, and I was able to hold you and breathe against your lips. I wanted you when you opened your eyes and looked at me, when you lay unconscious in the healer's home, when you first spoke my name. I want you all the time. I can think of very little else. Through everything, I have felt you in me, and it makes me more alive. You make this curse I am under bearable. I love you, Laurel. I want you for the rest of this eternity.'*

The honesty in his tone and the earnest expression in his eyes filled her with such hope and love that she had to kiss him. Her lips pressed against his. Their tongues touched, slipping beyond the borders to their lips. Not needing to pull away to speak, she said, '*I love you, too, Brutus.*'

The connection she felt to him was unlike anything she'd ever known. He swam backward as he kept her in his arms. His hair drifted around her.

'*Vitus?*' she asked.

'*With the healer. I do not think the arm can be saved,*' he said. '*Your coming saved him. You saved us both.*'

Laurel liked the approval she heard in his tone. 'I'm very happy to hear he's safe.'

Their tails skimmed against each other, sending a shiver over her. It was a strange sensation of pure emotion. Her love for him was there, but she had no burning sexual desire. It was probably just as well. She wasn't sure how sex with a tail and no noticeable sexual organs would work anyway.

'*I want to go home,*' she whispered.

'*I want to take you home,*' he answered. He pulled his mouth from hers and held her hand as he darted through the water. She had no choice but to trail behind him. The rush of current against her body was invigorating, and her heart pounded in excitement.

Suddenly remembering what she'd seen, she

began swishing her tail to help swim faster. *'Brutus, I saw mermaids in the water.'*

He stopped suddenly and led her down the rock base. *'Do you mean Demon and Brennus? Caderyn and Iason went looking for them to update them.'*

'No, mermaids. Women.'

'That's not possible. We sealed the only other exit.' He went into the surfacing area and held his hand out to pull her behind him.

'I got through,' she stated. *'Maybe someone—'*

Brutus broke the surface. *'You were already inside the palace. There was no way any of the Olympians made it inside, let alone through the halls to make it into the ocean.'*

He pulled up on the ledge and then bent over to lift her out of the water and set her down next to him. Whipping his tail around, he brushed the water off his legs. Laurel followed his example. Her body tingled, and she coughed as the taste of salt became more pronounced. Her tail pulled apart as she once again formed legs.

"I know what I saw," Laurel said. The wet material of her shirt stuck to her skin. The fins on her arms were slower to retract. "Three mermaids. One of them was talking, or think-talking, or mind-linking to the others about how the king couldn't keep them trapped inside and one was going to rule the dome."

"Maia. Was Lotis with her?"

Laurel frowned.

"Red hair. Red tail. Expression like she swam straight up from the bowels of a volcano?"

She nodded. "Yes. And one blonde, one dark brunette. The redhead talked about wanting to acquire replacement slaves to toy with and the leader said they needed to wait but would go soon."

"They found another way out." Brutus frowned. "That must have been what they were doing. They weren't trying to break the dome in an attempt to distract us with the earthquakes so they could make a new tunnel. They used the animals to cover up the noise."

"Can you find the tunnel and stop them?"

"We will try." He lifted his hand to her face and pushed her wet hair away from her cheek. "We would not have known this if you were not brave. Thank you."

"I was terrified," she admitted. "I think they sensed you coming. That is what kept me from being discovered. What will happen?"

"We will stop them again. It will not happen overnight, but it is no matter. We have been struggling with Maia and her followers since we were banished down here. The good news is, the earthquakes should stop, and the mermaids don't know we learned their secret." As the scales by his eyes became flesh, Brutus glanced down at his transformed lap. His cock stood proud and tall from his hips.

Laurel pulled the shirt over her head. Her body returned to normal and with that change came a rush of desire. A dam broke on her emotions, and she gasped in surprise at the sudden need in her sex. She instantly gravitated toward Brutus, straddling his lap on the surfacing room floor. Firm muscles rippled beneath her, still damp and cool from the ocean. The hard stone bit into her knees, but she didn't care. His shaft was erect and ready as it brushed up against her.

"What's happening?" she asked, before kissing him. His tongue slid over her lips, and she moaned. Hands grabbed hold of her thighs, squeezing tight, as Brutus rocked his hips against her.

"It's called the affliction," he answered between deep kisses. "It happens...whenever we come...out of the water."

He forcibly lifted her up to straddle him on the cave floor and drew her onto his shaft. The urgency of his desire was in his shaky movements. She pushed down. His hands slipped over her moist sides before taking hold of her breasts. He gripped them in his large palms as Laurel moved over him fast and hard.

"Mm, I like affliction." She covered his hands with hers.

The completely mindless drive she felt surpassed everything else. Nothing mattered except finishing what they started. Even with as desperate as she was to find release, her body seemed to tease her by keeping the orgasm just beyond her reach.

Laurel rode him harder, pounding her hips down. She gripped his shoulders to help her momentum. Brutus cupped her ass and in one swift movement rolled up from the floor until he was standing with her embedded on his cock. She held on as he walked to press her up against the wall. He took over, pumping his hips into her as he trapped her to the stone. The smell of cave flowers was strong. The sparkling reflection of the gem studded walls danced behind his head.

He carried her as if she weighed nothing. His muscles strained with each thrusting movement. The only tender thing in his claiming was his eyes, as he stared deeply into hers. Finally, the elusive orgasm came. She cried out in pleasure, but he didn't stop driving into her.

"I am going to find release in my wife," he whispered against her ear. "Say you're mine."

"Yours," she managed breathlessly.

His body jerked with an almost violent climax. He stiffened, pressed tight and deep into her. Holding her for a long moment, he then rocked a few more times in her wet depths before pulling out.

Laurel's legs could barely hold her as her feet touched the uneven floor next to the cave wall. Still trying to catch her breath, she said, "I really love the affliction."

He grinned. "I really love you, my lady."

In that moment, nothing else mattered, not mermaids and secret tunnels, because somehow, she knew everything would be all right as long as she was in the arms of the man she loved. Together, they could face anything. Smiling softly, she responded, "I really love you, too."

The End

THE SERIES CONTINUES...

The Mighty Hunter
Commanding the Tides
Captive of the Deep
Surrender to the Sea
Making Waves
The Merman King

Making Waves
Lords of the Abyss Book 5

When Demon, a merman tasked with patrolling the ocean for humans in distress, comes across a woman anchored to the bottom of the sea, he's sure his dreams have come true. After all, she's stunning, single, and makes his body burn with need. She's also impetuous, being hunted by his enemies, and seriously conflicted on whether or not he's a good guy. It's his duty to not only protect her, but to win her heart—because this lonely merman is sure she's the one for him. Now he just has to convince her of as much.

Excerpt

This was hell.

Victoria had no doubts about that simple fact. The rental boat she'd taken out on vacation had sunk, she'd drowned, and for her sins she'd been sent to hell. It wasn't fire and brimstone. It was the endless abyss, the dark depths of the ocean—cold and lonely and wet.

She was trapped at the bottom of the world, impossibly aware of her surroundings, unable to breathe anything but the salty brine. It turned out heaven wasn't as lenient as some would have her believe, because a greater power had condemned her into the watery sea for playing a little too loose with her tax deductions, and calling Becky Gibson a bitch in the third grade, and any number of things she had considered small infractions at the time.

Sorry Becky.

And she found she *was* sorry. Victoria had a lot of time to think about it. She was sorry for a great many things these days. Or weeks? She couldn't be sure. Time was not kept in the deep ocean, not like onshore.

Something flitted by her vision and she stiffened. Victoria waited, the sickening feeling curling through her stomach to tell her that this was it—some grand finale to end her horrible journey through death. The monsters were going to come nibble on her again—horrible little fish with sharp teeth and glowing dots hanging from their heads. All she could do was thrash about until they went away or she became too tired to fight.

She'd seen a couple of larger creatures, but they thankfully stayed in the distance, passing like shadows within a shadow. Tentacles skimmed sand, stirring clouds that looked like nightmares. She had to concentrate in the darkness to see them, her eyesight focused like the beams of two flashlights with a limited field of vision.

Other creatures crawled beneath her through the

pasture of flowing seagrass...or was it moss, or a fungus that crawled up from dark places? Once, a line of translucent lobsters with giant claws had marched past. She felt more than saw them, but tried not to move, not wanting them to notice her floating in the abyss like a meal on a string. Long, thin worms drifted with the currents and she tried to avoid touching them.

The fear of things she couldn't see was worse than the dangers lurking in the waters.

Demons.

They called themselves Olympians and acted like goddesses, but Victoria found nothing godly about their glowing eyes and unnatural coloring, or the way they'd pulled her into the water to drown her a second time—as if the first death had not been enough torture. They'd said many things when they'd held her prisoner at Mt. Olympus, but she'd been so dazed, coming in and out of focus as they spoke, that very little had registered.

Yep. This is hell, and the Ancient Greeks run it.

And the ugly fish with their razor teeth.

And the darkness. Endless darkness.

Victoria had become a strange and slimy plant. She was tethered by her waist, fastened to the seabed with a thick chain that was her stem. And her leaves were the silky fins where her feet used to be. She missed her feet. She missed her legs. Now there was a fish tail—useless because she couldn't even kick with it.

In the distance, she detected a large dome, sunken into the water like a snow globe some kid had dropped and forgotten. The Olympian demons who had planted her said that she should try to make it back to the dome, like a test rigged for her to fail. Yet, it was her only chance at salvation.

Well, *said* was too incorrect of a word. They didn't use their mouths to speak. Instead they implanted the thoughts of what they were saying in her head.

The best Victoria could reason is that if she made it to the dome, she'd become a demon like the women who'd brought her here. They all had tails, too. Had they been like her once? A lost soul trying to reason with the unknown?

Her thoughts drifted like ocean currents, making it harder for her to quantify events so she could fathom what had happened. Conclusions came to her, but it was as if they'd already been formed and forgotten like waves that had been washed ashore, useless, and pointless upon reflection.

Mermaids? Demons?

Was she a mermaid? She looked at her tail, and then at the ugly fins that jutted from her once smooth arms.

The light from the dome caught her attention yet again and her thoughts drifted to salvation. Familiar darkness or the light of the unknown?

Anything was better than the constant fear residing in her chest, and the oppressive icy silence of ocean water.

Deep ocean. Mortals don't come here. Therefore, I am not mortal, she thought.

Victoria flung her arms back and forth, trying to pull herself through the water. Each inch was hard fought. After she managed to move several feet, she couldn't pump her arms anymore. Water entered and expelled from her lungs, the feeling heavy and uncomfortable. She fought to move again, resting and fighting, fighting and resting. Two feet. Four feet. One foot. An inch.

Victoria opened her mouth to scream, but the water kept her in silence.

No more.

Please, no more.

I'm sorry, Becky.

I didn't mean to cheat on my test, Mrs. Larsen. I swear I saw the answer by accident.

I'll clean my room.

I'm sorry I threw away perfectly good food. I know other kids are starving and would be grateful for your tuna noodle casserole, Mom.

I miss my parents. I'll call them more often.

I'll not take deductions on my taxes.

I'll not swear, or watch bad movies, or drink, or tell indecent jokes.

I'll volunteer more.

So many sins...

No more, please.

I don't know what else there could be.

No more.

To find out more about Michelle's books
visit www.MichellePillow.com

New York Times & *USA TODAY*
Bestselling Author

Michelle loves to travel and try new things, whether it's a paranormal investigation of an old Vaudeville Theatre or climbing Mayan temples in Belize. She believes life is an adventure fueled by copious amounts of coffee.

Newly relocated to the American South, Michelle is involved in various film and documentary projects with her talented director husband. She is mom to a fantastic artist. And she's managed by a dog and cat who make sure she's meeting her deadlines.

For the most part she can be found wearing pajama pants and working in her office. There may or may not be dancing. It's all part of the creative process.

**Come say hello! Michelle loves talking
with readers on social media!**

www.MichellePillow.com

facebook.com/AuthorMichellePillow

twitter.com/michellepillow

instagram.com/michellempillow

bookbub.com/authors/michelle-m-pillow

goodreads.com/Michelle_Pillow

amazon.com/author/michellepillow

youtube.com/michellepillow

pinterest.com/michellepillow

COMPLIMENTARY EXCERPTS

THE DRAGON'S QUEEN

BY MICHELLE M. PILLOW

Dragon Lords Series

Bestselling Shape-shifter Romance

Mede of the Draig knows three things for a fact: As the only female dragon-shifter of her people, she is special. She can kick the backside of any man. And she absolutely doesn't want to marry.

Mede has spent a lifetime trying to prove herself as strong as any male warrior. Unfortunately, being the special, rare creature she is, she's been claimed as the future bride to nearly three dozen Draig—each one confident that when they come for her hand in marriage fate will choose them. When the men aren't bragging about how they're going to marry her, they're acting like she's a delicate rare flower in need of their protection.

She is far from a shrinking solarflower.

Prince Llyr of the Draig knows four things for a fact: He is the future king of the dragon-shifters. He must act honorably in all ways. He absolutely, positively is meant to marry Lady Mede. And she dead set against marriage.

Llyr's fate rests in the hands of a woman determined not to have any man. With a new threat emerging amongst their cat-shifting neighbors, a threat whose eyes are focused firmly on Mede, time may be running out. It is up to him to convince her to be his dragon queen.

The Dragon's Queen Extended Excerpt

Mede's lungs expanded with the effort of a hard run. Morning crept over the horizon, brightening the light of night. In one hand she gripped Rolant's knife, and in the other, her prize. For a moment, she felt perfection in the burn of her legs, the pant of her breath, the rhythm of her feet. When she jumped over forest debris, she flew.

The exercise felt wonderful, but not nearly as wonderful as the sounds of cheers coming from the border. They had lit a fire to guide her back and she ran toward it. As she neared the group of dragons she leapt over the border. Lifting her hand, she yelled, "Dragons!"

"Dragons!" the men yelled, celebrating her victorious run.

Mede turned the hilt of the knife toward Rolant to return the blade. He took it. Instantly, his smile faded as he saw the blood. His eyes roamed her as she let the dragon-shift fade from her body. Before he could ask her about it, she proudly lifted her fist balled around the fur. "Victory!"

"Victory!" the men yelled, clearly well into their cups. While she had her adventure, they'd partied.

"Our lady found the still," Arthur said, with a laugh as he sniffed the liquor fumes on her. The man had a crook to his nose from having been punched a few too many times. When he drank, he liked to brawl.

"How is the mangy cat?" Cynan asked.

"Owain remembers you fondly," Mede answered, grinning. A round of shouts and laughter cut off the conversation. After it finally died down, she held out her hand. "My prize."

A few of the men looked down at her outstretched hand, then a couple more. Their laughter died as they took in her achievement.

"That doesn't look like..." Saben gave her a questioning look.

Dylan reached to pinch a bit of the fur. "It's blond."

"Mede?" Rolant inquired, clearly wishing she'd explain. "Didn't you find the still?"

"Yes, but I wanted a harder target," she said. "Besides, the still farmer was already missing a lot of tufts. I felt sorry for him."

Rolant lifted the blade, showing the blood to the others. "Who did you fight?"

Mede thought of the stranger. There was no reason to tell them what had happened. They didn't need to know the cat-shifter had kissed her. That would be her secret.

"We didn't exchange names." She gave a little shrug of dismissal.

"Test it, so none my challenge her claim," Rolant said. There was a lot of fumbling as they searched for a particular satchel that held the genetic testing fluid. As the others were distracted, Rolant pulled her aside. "I sent you to the still farmer. What were you thinking? The only blond Var I have seen belong to the elite palace guard. That or the prince. How did you get it? Why is there blood on—?"

"It's good!" Dylan yelled, lifting a small vial to pour testing liquid onto the ground. When the cat-shifter fur combined with the chemicals it turned the test liquid a pale blue color. "It's Var."

"Not now, Rolant," Mede said. "I need a drink."

A bottle was instantly shoved in her direction. She drank deeply of the liquor. It stung her throat and warmed her belly.

"Tell us of the run," Cynan said.

"What's this?" a male voice boomed over the encampment.

Mede was relieved for it saved her from having to tell that particular fireside story.

"Do you have permission to be on my land?" the stranger continued.

Mede lowered the bottle and wiped her mouth on her sleeve. She didn't recognize the voice. Several of the men blocked her view. Since they camped on palace land with Prince Rolant she wasn't too concerned by the claim.

"Brother!" Rolant acknowledged. "You've returned. I thought you were hunting yorkins."

"Gildas was injured. Nothing serious, but we decided to bring him home so he could have the proper medical attention," Prince Llyr answered.

Mede changed her mind. She didn't like the interruption. This was her victory morning. She didn't want to meet a new male Draig, and certainly not the heir prince. The prince was not married and had already told Rolant he wanted to meet her.

"Hand me a drink," Llyr said. "Whose victory are we celebrating?"

Like grasses being blown aside by a stout wind, the men parted to let Llyr see her. She stiffened and automatically lifted her jaw. "Mine."

"You?" Llyr repeated in disbelief. He looked at Rolant for confirmation. "And she passed?"

"And we saw her fly," Saben inserted.

"That was you who flew," Arthur said.

"Oh, right." Saben nodded. He lifted his cup and announced. "And I flew!"

"How is Owain?" Llyr asked.

"In need of a bath," Mede said.

"She brought back blond fur," Rolant stated.

"Blond...?" Llyr handed the bottle he held to his brother and stepped forward to look at her.

Mede was glad she smelled like a liquor still and sweat. And she probably looked like a wild beast after her run. She forced herself not to look at his chest to see his crystal. Looking at his face was worse.

In many ways he reminded her of Rolant, only his eyes were a brighter green—so bright they penetrated her, taking her in as if he could see all her secrets. Mede didn't like to feel exposed. His light brown hair hung to his chin whereas Rolant's was much longer. She thought of the kiss the Var had stolen from her. She had not been expecting it and really had felt nothing but surprise when it happened, but the memory caused her eyes to dart down to Llyr's mouth.

"Finally we meet, Lady Medellyn," he said.

Mede forced her eyes away from his firm lips. She swallowed nervously. "I am called Mede. And I am not a lady. Today I am a Dead Dragon."

At the words the inebriated men cheered. "Dead Dragons!"

Llyr chuckled. More to himself than to her, he said, "I can see the liquor has not gone to waste here."

"If you'll excuse me, prince, I want my scar." She made a move to leave his presence, still refusing to look down. The idea that a prince would be her mate terrified her. She'd never wanted this meeting.

"Wait," Llyr said, being so bold as to grab her

arm. "I should like to congratulate you on a good run."

Mede arched a brow. The more she found herself mesmerized by his eyes, the more stubborn her demeanor became. When he didn't speak, she said, "Well?"

"Congratulations on a good run," he answered softly.

"Thank you, prince," she answered dutifully before moving to skirt past him. The men had started to sing a bawdy song as they linked arms and began a noisy, drunken chain through the campsite. The prancing took them away from where she stood. She wished they'd circle back.

Llyr grabbed her arm again. "Did you really take the fur from a member of the royal court?"

At the time she hadn't been nervous, but now, the way both Llyr and Rolant mentioned the fur color, made her suddenly a little sick to her stomach. Nerves bunched in her chest and she nodded once. "I suppose I did though at the time I didn't ask for his name."

"What did he look like?"

"A cat," she answered, being difficult on purpose. His fingers lingered on her arm, the touch somehow intimate. Finally she got the nerve to look down. At first, she thought she might have seen a soft glow in the stone. Only on the festival night would it light to full power. She stiffened, until she realized that it must have been firelight reflection. He was not her mate. A sigh of relief whispered past her lips... followed by a sense of disappointment. The disappointment confused her and made her want to run away like a coward.

"Have you mated?" Llyr asked, eyeing her neck.

Always to that.

She lowered her eyes over her lashes. "I have no interest in marriage. I would like my scar though." She tried to pull her arm.

He tightened his grip. "So it is true. You broke your own crystal. Why?"

Mede grimaced, remembering that day long ago. Her mother had wept openly for months over it. "So did you." She reached for his chest, pinching the crystal from where it laid against him and gave it a little toss. It bounced against him. An almost microscopic thin crack marred the inside of the stone.

"An accident when I was a boy trick riding ceffyls," Llyr said.

"My father is a ceffyl breeder. You should not be trick riding them," she lectured. "They are in delicate supply and not for games."

"I was a boy," he stated, enunciating the words. His attitude infuriated her.

"No excuse," she answered just as arrogantly.

"I broke my arm, if that helps."

"It's a start." She again tried to pull her arm free from his grasp.

The singing had reached the forest and the men disappeared behind a colossal tree. Somehow being alone with him made her nervous.

"Unhand me, prince," she said at last. "I earned my place here."

Llyr looked at her arm in surprise, as if he didn't know he held her. Instantly his fingers released her. "Tell me first, why did you crush your crystal?"

"What? I love me. I married myself." She wasn't sure why she was being obstinate or sarcastic. All she knew is that her arm tingled where he touched her. She glanced at his stone. It didn't glow. Still, the urge to run from him was great. Her muscles felt weak. Surely her body shook from the long night of exercise, nothing else. Her mind felt fuzzy because she was tired. It had nothing to do with his smell or those eyes. Those damned green eyes.

"Somehow I don't think you're truly that narcissistic, my lady."

"Very well. If you must know, it is because I

make my own fate." Mede gave a little hop past him and went to join the dancing men. Saben and Cynan broke the chain to let her in. As they pulled her away from the prince, she was glad for the escape. Something about the man drew her in and frustrated the netherworld out of her. She was pretty sure it was his eyes. No man should ever possess eyes like that.

To find out more about Michelle's books visit www.MichellePillow.com

LOVE POTIONS

BY MICHELLE M. PILLOW

Warlocks MacGregor® Book 1
Contemporary Paranormal Scottish Warlocks

A little magickal mischief never hurt anyone...

Erik MacGregor, from a clan of ancient Scottish
warlocks, isn't looking for love. After centuries, it's
not even a consideration...until he moves in next door
to Lydia Barratt. It's clear that the shy beauty wants
nothing to do with him, but he's drawn to her none-
theless and determined to win her over.

Lydia Barratt just wants to be left alone to grow
flowers and make lotions in her old Victorian house.
The last thing she needs is a demanding Scottish
man meddling in her private life. Just because he's

gorgeous and totally rocks a kilt doesn't mean she's going to fall for his seductive manner.

But Erik won't give up and just as Lydia let's her guard down, his sister decides to get involved. Her little love potion prank goes terribly wrong, making Lydia the target of his sudden embarrassingly obsessive behavior. They'll have to find a way to pull Erik out of the spell fast when it becomes clear that Lydia has more than a lovesick warlock to worry about. Evil lurks within the shadows and it plans to use Lydia, alive or dead, to take out Erik and his clan for good.

Love Potions Excerpt

"Ly-di-ah! I sit beneath your window, laaaass, singing 'cause I loooove your a—"''

"For the love of St. Francis of Assisi, someone call a vet. There is an injured animal screaming in pain outside," Charlotte interrupted the flow of music in ill-humor.

Lydia lifted her forehead from the kitchen table. Her windows and doors were all locked, and yet Erik's endlessly verbose singing penetrated the barrier of glass and wood with ease.

Charlotte held her head and blinked heavily. Her red-rimmed eyes were filled with the all too poignant look of a hangover. She took a seat at the table and laid her head down. Her moan sounded something like, "I'm never moving again."

"You need fluids," Lydia prescribed, getting up to pour unsweetened herbal tea from the pitcher in the fridge. She'd mixed it especially for her friend. It was Gramma Annabelle's hangover recipe of willow bark, peppermint, carrot, and ginger. The old lady always had a fresh supply of it in the house while she was alive. Apparently, being a natural witch also meant in partaking in natural liquors. Annabelle had kept a steady supply of moonshine stashed in the basement. If the concert didn't stop soon she might try to find an old bottle.

"Ly-di-ah!"

"Omigod. Kill me," Charlotte moaned. "No. Kill him. Then kill me."

"Ly-di-ah!"

Erik had been singing for over an hour. At first, he'd tried to come inside. She'd not invited him and the barrier spell sent him sprawling back into the yard. He didn't seem to mind as he found a seat on some landscaping timbers and began his serenade. The last time she'd asked him to be quiet, he'd gotten louder and overly enthusiastic. In fact, she'd been too scared to pull back the curtains for a clearer look, but she was pretty sure he'd been dancing on her lawn, shaking his kilt.

"Omigod," Charlotte muttered, pushing up and angrily going to a window. Then grimacing, she said, "Is he wearing a tux jacket with his kilt?"

"Don't let him see you," Lydia cried out in a panic. It was too late. The song began with renewed force.

"He's..." Charlotte frowned. "I think it's dancing."

Since the damage was done, Lydia joined Charlotte at the window. Erik grinned. He lifted his arms to the side and kicked his legs, bouncing around the yard like a kid on too much sugar. "Maybe it's a traditional Scottish dance?"

Both women tilted their heads in unison as his kilt kicked up to show his perfectly formed ass.

"He's not wearing..." Charlotte began.

"I know. He doesn't," Lydia answered. Damn, the man had a fine body. Too bad Malina's trick had turned him insane.

To find out more about Michelle's books visit www.MichellePillow.com

PLEASE LEAVE A REVIEW
THANK YOU FOR READING!

Please take a moment to share your thoughts by reviewing this book.

Be sure to check out Michelle's other titles at www.MichellePillow.com

www.ingramcontent.com/pod-product-compliance
Lightning Source LLC
Chambersburg PA
CBHW030636120726
47904CB00006B/2176